THE DOCTOR'S VISITOR

Alice Grey

CHIVERS

British Library Cataloguing in Publication Data available

This Large Print edition published by BBC Audiobooks Ltd, Bath, 2009.
Published by arrangement with the author.

U.K. Hardcover ISBN 978 1 408 41203 9
U.K. Softcover ISBN 978 1 408 41204 6

Printed and bound in Great Britain by CPI Antony Rowe, Chippenham
and Eastbourne

To the memory of my mother and father.
With love.

CHAPTER ONE

Leigh glanced at the sky as she left Simpson's tea-shop in Stow-on-the-Wold, wondering if the rain would keep off. Walking towards the Green, she found herself behind a small group of people, mainly middle-aged and elderly women. Only two of the group were elderly men—husbands, more than likely, thought Leigh. They chatted between themselves as they meandered slowly past the White Hart behind the others.

Leigh glanced at her watch. Ten-thirty. She'd just make it to Birmingham by twelve if the traffic was fairly light. She moved into the road to overtake the leisurely group, and it was as she passed the two men, straggling behind, that something made her glance at one of them. She wasn't sure if it was the fact that he looked remarkably like her late father, or the way he put his hand to his throat and seemed to sway. As if in slow motion, she saw him reach out to grasp his friend's sleeve, and noticed the look of pain and fear that crossed his features. Before he had even crumpled into a heap on the damp pavement, she had reached his side, her fingers feeling for his pulse.

The man's face had been pale, then grey, now it was a dusky blue. Someone else was

1

kneeling at his other side, and his hand seemed almost to tear the jacket open.

'Someone fetch an ambulance! Quickly—it's urgent!' The young man's voice held authority, and Leigh was aware of someone hurrying away across the Green. The man was not breathing. Quickly she ran a finger around the inside of his mouth. No obstruction. Not looking at the other first-aider, she lifted the man's chin and closed off his nostrils.

'That's right. You do the mouth-to-mouth. I'll do the cardiac compressions. Come on, give him some air!'

A little disconcerted by his peremptory tone, Leigh breathed three times quickly into the man's mouth, watching as his chest rose and fell. Long, lean fingers rested briefly on the man's neck, then the heels of his hands began to press firmly and sharply over the man's still heart. Leigh breathed again into his mouth. Five compressions, one breath, just as they had been taught in Casualty. They seemed to be working well as a team. The young man—and a brief glance revealed fair hair and blue eyes—had obviously been well trained too. His movements were confident and practised. He must have done this before, Leigh decided.

He laid his fingers on the man's neck. Leigh had gradually become aware of the low murmuring from the crowd that had gathered. One woman was softly crying, others were comforting her.

'Ssh, Meg, they're doing all they can. He'll be all right.' Leigh doubted the wisdom of that remark, but was too busy to argue.

'His colour's better,' someone else whispered.

'I don't think it's working,' wailed Meg softly. 'What am I going to do?'

Leigh breathed into his mouth again, her eyes vaguely registering mud on her skirt. She glanced up at the fair-haired man. His fingers rested on the man's pulse.

'We're nearly there. Once more.' They repeated the routine. Leigh laid her own fingers on the man's neck. And suddenly—a pulse was there! Her own heart seemed to lurch in sympathy. The man's chest rose of its own accord. He stirred, and gave a little groan. His eyes flickered.

'Oh—thank God!' cried the woman called Meg. 'He's awake!'

The sound of a siren filled the air, then an ambulance almost skidded to a halt a few yards away. Leigh scrambled to her feet. Her job was done. The fair-haired man began talking in a low voice to the ambulance attendants. Meg kneeled beside her husband, tears running down her face. The patient—who did look remarkably like Leigh's father—was murmuring to her.

With the sense of a job well done, Leigh left the group and walked across to her car, parked in the Square. The young man could give them all the details. He seemed very competent. As she took out her keys, her gaze still on the group of people, now dispersing, and the stretcher being lifted into the ambulance, the young man left them and walked briskly over to her.

'You did very well,' he commented. She opened her car door.

'I could say the same for you. Have you done it before?'

He shrugged his shoulders. 'Once or twice. You?'

'No. But I was taught well. And I'm a nurse.'

His mouth twisted wryly. 'Oh, I see. Then you'd be bound to be good.'

She wondered if he was being sarcastic, but his face was straight. 'I'm afraid I have to—' She brushed at her muddy skirt.

'Which is your hospital?' he asked. He had a deep, pleasant voice, and now she realised he wasn't quite as young as she'd first thought. Probably at least thirty. A nice family man, she imagined.

'I don't work in a hospital,' she explained. 'I'm a health visitor—in Bath. That is, I'm leaving Bath—for a while, anyway—and I've got an interview today, and just look at the mess I'm in now!'

She rubbed at the hem of her grey pin-striped suit, and hoped she'd got a cloth or something in the car, to rub the mud off the

4

toes of her best black court shoes.

'So where are you going now?' Was he really as interested as he seemed, or was she imagining things?

'Birmingham. Well, the outskirts of Birmingham.'

'You'd better tell me your name.'

She blinked. 'Why should I tell you my name?'

'Well, I'm sure the man's wife—Meg—will want to write and thank you for saving her husband's life.'

'He isn't out of the wood yet,' she said curtly. 'We may have only postponed the inevitable.'

He smiled, showing white, even teeth, and a long dimple in his cheek.

'Even so. It will ease her conscience.'

'You'd better have my mother's address,' she murmured, writing it down on a small notepad he produced from his pocket. He glanced at it as he retrieved his pen—an expensive Waterman, she noticed.

'Leigh Rochester. Most unusual. Mmm, Mossgate.'

His blue eyes seemed to be searching her face, analysing the expression in her dark-lashed hazel eyes. She felt awkward.

'You've heard of it?' she asked.

'Yes, I have.' He held out his hand. 'We may meet again, Miss Rochester. Er—it is *Miss* Rochester, I take it?'

She flushed at his tone, and the firm pressure of his fingers.

'At the moment—yes.'

He released her hand quickly. 'I see. Well, my name's Adam. It's been nice talking to you.'

With a brief smile he turned and strode quickly away, along to Parson's Corner, and out of sight. Slowly, thoughtfully, Leigh opened the door of her car. There was something about him, something she'd seen in other men—in other men she'd liked. But she'd probably never see this particular man again. Pity.

*   *   *

It was a quarter to one by the clock on her dashboard when Leigh turned off the main Oxford road in Mossgate, into Hillwood Avenue, and pulled into the small car park in front of the health centre. She'd intended to arrive before lunch, but the diversion in Stow-on-the-Wold had delayed her by at least half an hour. She hoped they hadn't given up waiting for her, and started their lunch. That wouldn't augur well for the future. Late for her first interview!

Although she'd lived most of her life in Mossgate, she didn't know the layout of the health centre. It was large, purpose-built, and quite new, and she'd been away for seven

6

years. She pushed open the wide glass door, and paused to tuck a stray piece of nut-brown hair behind her ear. She hoped the damp patch at the hem of her skirt didn't show too much. She read the signs on the wall ahead: 'Patients' Toilets'. 'Surgeries'. 'Dental Surgery'. 'Health Visitors'. She could see a large window to her left, and behind it a number of uniformed receptionists were busily making appointments, answering the phone, looking for files. She followed the last sign and turned right. 'Toilets'. 'Health Visitors'. She knocked the door. There was no reply. She knocked again.

'Did you want somebody, love?' A plump, middle-aged woman in a pink overall poked her head around a door further along.

'Miss Horton. Is she around?' asked Leigh.

'Oh, I expect she's 'aving 'er lunch. Twelve-thirty on the dot—you could set your clocks by her. Are you one of 'er families?'

Leigh smiled. 'No. I have an appointment, but I was—delayed. My name's Rochester. I've come from—'

'Ah, you're the young lady from Bath!' The woman came into the corridor, wiping her hands on her overall. She thrust one out at Leigh, who held it, smiling. 'I'm Edna. I'm a sort of clinic nurse. I was just clearing up after the Well Babies when you knocked. Come on, I'll take you through to the kitchen. I bet you'd like a cuppa after your journey.'

She led Leigh back to a door quite near the front door.

'I did stop at Stow,' Leigh began to explain, but Edna didn't hear her and pushed the door open with a grand air.

'This is Miss Rochester from Bath,' she announced. Leigh felt embarrassed, as three pairs of eyes turned to look at her.

'I'm sorry I'm late—' she began, but the nearest person was already on her feet and coming to meet her.

'I'd almost given up on you, Miss Rochester,' she said, but her words were spoken amiably. 'Were you delayed?'

'I was, actually. In Stow. A man was taken ill—a coronary.'

'Really?'

Leigh was aware of keen but friendly grey eyes behind the gold-rimmed spectacles, and a springy sort of tension in the lean, muscular frame. She wore a rather shapeless brown tweed skirt and a mustard-coloured twin-set that had seen better days.

'What did you do?' asked one of the other women eagerly. She was a heavily built girl with a mass of frizzy red hair and pale eyes that shone excitedly.

'Well, I did mouth-to-mouth, and cardiac compression—just what anyone would have—'

'You saved his life!' exclaimed the red-haired girl. 'How exciting! Do you know, all the years I've been nursing, and I've never

8

been called on to save someone's life. It's always someone else.'

'Thank your lucky stars, then, Pauline,' said the first woman sharply, and held out a hand to Leigh. 'I'm Daphne Horton. This is Pauline Morris.' Pauline grasped Leigh's hand and pumped it up and down. 'And this is Ros Wentworth, our clinic doctor.'

The third person present reached across the back of the chair, and coolly held Leigh's hand for a moment. She was round-faced, blonde, and rosy-cheeked, and looked more like a milkmaid than a doctor, thought Leigh.

'And this is Leigh Rochester,' said Daphne Horton to the others. 'Replacement for Carol.'

'I thought she was named Maureen or something,' said Ros smilingly, glancing at Leigh's slim figure in her grey suit.

'Didn't I tell you?' said Daphne. 'Maureen went off sick.'

'She was only part-time, anyway,' said Pauline, returning to her seat by the radiator. 'And she was only here for a week.'

'This is neither here nor there,' said Daphne Horton, tugging at her jumper. 'I don't know about you, Miss Rochester, but I'm anxious for my lunch.'

'Oh, please don't—' Leigh began.

'I shan't starve,' said Daphne shortly. 'I dare say I can wait. Off you go, Edna, and finish what you were doing. I'm quite capable of making Miss Rochester a cup of tea later.'

'That's all right,' Leigh hurried to reassure her. 'I shall be going home afterwards—that is, to my mother's house—for lunch. She's expecting me.'

'Your mother? Oh, of course, yes—Arthur said—' Colour tinged Daphne's cheeks. 'Well, I'd better show you round, Miss Rochester, introduce you to the doctors. I think you'll get on with Dr Christie.'

'I take it we're GP attached here?' queried Leigh.

'Oh, yes, always have been. Adam Christie's particularly keen on psychology, so you'd better brush it up.'

Leigh gave a little laugh. 'I'll certainly do that. Er—did you say *Adam* Christie?'

'Do you know him? I wasn't aware he'd ever worked in Bath.'

'Oh, no, I don't know him.'

But her mention of the name Adam had immediately given her a vision of a blond-haired man doing cardiac compressions extremely competently. She couldn't stop the sudden rush of colour to her cheeks, and was relieved when Pauline got up, saying eagerly, 'I could show Miss Rochester round, if you want your lunch, Daphne.'

Daphne turned to her. 'It's quite all right, Pauline. You finish yours. Right.' She turned briskly to Leigh. 'I'll show you our office first.' She took Leigh by the arm and led her back into the large waiting hall and down another

10

small corridor. The first door was marked 'Ladies', the second, 'Health Visitors'. Leigh followed Daphne inside and was shown her desk, next to Pauline's. Daphne's own desk overlooked a small, rather weedy garden, and the pram park.

'About your contract,' said Daphne, sitting. Leigh followed suit. 'You know it's just for six months, don't you? Maternity leave for Carol. She's an excellent health visitor, got married last year. I did think she might have waited a bit longer before starting a family, but there you are. She's in her thirties, so I suppose she couldn't afford to wait. She's due back next April.'

'She's already left, hasn't she? Did she fall ill?' asked Leigh.

'No, that was Maureen. Carol left early with hypertension, and we got Maureen from an agency. But she went down with glandular fever—pretty bad, too. We were really stuck, Pauline and I both trying to do Carol's families as well as our own.' She pulled a face.

'I suppose the least urgent got left,' murmured Leigh.

'Indeed they did not!' said Daphne indignantly. 'But we were working all hours. Sylvia couldn't help much. She's part-time, four mornings a week, but she's married, with three children, so we couldn't ask her to help.'

Leigh formed a distinct impression that Daphne was not in favour of married health

11

visitors with commitments.

'Arthur,' Daphne went on, 'that's Dr Brent—we're very informal here—he'd been to see your mother, and she mentioned you were a health visitor looking for a job—'

'I wasn't, really. I had—have—a good job down in Bath, but my sister normally looks after my mother, and she's moving down—'

'Of course, that's it—she's going down to Swindon, isn't she, and your mother's disabled? A stroke?'

'It's Oxford, actually. And my mother had a brain operation ten years ago, which left her with a left hemiplegia. She's greatly improved, though. Not much paralysis now, just a weakness.'

'She ought to come to our disabled club on Tuesdays,' said Daphne. 'We've got Graham running it now. He's very good. He likes the elderly.'

'My mother isn't elderly, she's only fifty-six. And I'm afraid she doesn't like to think of herself as disabled. She's convinced she'll be completely cured one day.'

'After ten years? She's very optimistic.'

'It's not optimism,' Leigh explained. 'She just refuses to look at painful facts, I'm afraid.'

'Aren't we all a bit like that? Do bring her along, Miss Rochester—may we call you Leigh?'

'By all means. Well, I'll ask her, but I'm not sure if she'll agree.'

12

'She can walk a little?' asked Daphne.

'With a stick. She can do most simple things for herself, and Kate says she potters about in the house—a little cooking, a bit of polishing. She can't do shopping or heavy things—Kate's always done that. We were rather surprised when John, my brother-in-law, was offered his promotion, but it meant moving away. And someone has to stay with Mother, so I decided to come back. It's seven years since I lived at home.'

'Does your sister have children?'

'A boy, Ricky. He's eleven. They've lived with Mother most of their married life, because Ricky was just a baby when Mother had her accident. Fortunately, it's a largish house, so there's plenty of room.'

'Banbury Road, isn't it? Yes, they're very nice houses. Doesn't your father help your mother?' Daphne asked.

'He died eight years ago—heart attack.' Leigh tightened her lips, recalling the incident in Stow earlier in the day. Meg had been fortunate that someone had been around who knew what to do. Her father hadn't been so lucky.

'I take it your mother doesn't want to move to Oxford with your sister,' Daphne queried.

'It would be impossible just yet,' Leigh explained. 'Kate and John have only been able to get a small flat for the time being. They're hoping to get something larger when they're

13

settled.'

'How will your mother cope with your being out most of the day?'

'I shall go home for lunch. And I shall be there in the evenings, and during the weekends. She's not helpless. And she has the phone. It was fortunate, I suppose, that it was a left-sided hemiplegia, so her speech was never affected.'

Daphne smiled and nodded. Leigh glanced at her. 'I think your Tuesday club may be just what she needs. I've tried to persuade Kate to encourage her to do more, but I suppose, Kate not having medical knowledge, she's always pampered Mother, never let her forget what a serious operation it was.'

'A tumour?'

'Yes, but it wasn't diagnosed until she had an accident, and a head injury. I always felt it should have been diagnosed earlier, and the doctor at the hospital felt the same—' Leigh swallowed, smiled at Daphne. 'It was a young doctor, I suppose, newly qualified—a locum GP. It's better forgotten, don't you agree?'

'A bit late for recriminations,' nodded Daphne.

'Although I suppose it would be—interesting—profitable—' Leigh searched for the right word '—gratifying, if we ever did find out what really happened, why it was never suspected. I suppose we'll never know.' She shrugged.

'Wouldn't help your mother now,' said Daphne.

'No,' said Leigh. 'So that's it,' she ended rather lamely. 'I've come back to stay with Mother, and once Kate's got a proper house Mother can go and live with them again, and I can go back to Bath.'

'You're planning to go back to Bath when you've finished here?'

'My job's being kept open for me. And I have friends there.'

'A boyfriend, I suppose.'

'No, just friends.' But she couldn't help thinking of Colin. He was very fond of her, she knew that. Quite serious, in fact. Far too serious about everything, not really her type at all. But so nice and kind. And she wasn't in love with him.

'Supposing your mother isn't able to move down to Oxford before next April?' suggested Daphne.

'I shall cross that bridge when I come to it. A lot can happen in six months.'

'It can.' Daphne stood up. 'Well, I think that's enough talking. At least, my stomach tells me it is. I'll show you around the centre. Although you probably know what it's like.'

'I don't, actually. I've only visited here about twice, and that was before I left to do my general training. It was fairly new then, built just before my mother's accident. She used to see Dr Williams—but he'd been away at the time, so she saw his locum—' Leigh was aware she'd been musing aloud, and caught Daphne's eyes on her.

'Dr Williams?' echoed Daphne, as they left the room to begin their tour. 'He retired two years ago. Dr Brent took over his practice. I'm Dr Brent's health visitor.'

Again, two spots of colour burned in her cheeks. Leigh noticed it without comment.

'How many doctors to each health visitor?' she asked as they reached the hall again.

'Two, I'm afraid. You'll take the families of Dr Christie and Dr Powell. Dr Powell's a lady—she specialises in gynaecology and obstetrics. Dr Christie—well, I told you, didn't I? Psychiatry's his pet. Come on.'

It was rather a rushed visit, and Leigh suspected Daphne's stomach was dictating the brevity. There were quick hellos to district nurses and a district midwife; the dentist gave them a quick smile, and the receptionist waved to them. Privately, Leigh thought the place was a maze, and was sure she'd never find her way around the labyrinth of rooms—waiting-rooms, surgeries, offices.

They were just about to enter the last room, where the Tuesday club was held, when Daphne paused as a tall figure entered the centre, dressed in brown checked trousers and a green corduroy jacket. Her face lit up. Leigh felt hot colour flood into her cheeks, and turned away. What on earth was he doing here? Had he followed her?

Daphne waved to him. 'Dr Christie!' He smiled and approached them. 'I'm so glad you're here, Dr Christie,' said Daphne warmly. 'This is your new health visitor.'

CHAPTER TWO

Leigh was forced to turn and look at him. His blue eyes were twinkling as they met her own hazel ones. Was he laughing at her?

'Good afternoon, Dr Christie,' she said coolly.

'I thought we might meet again,' he said smoothly, holding out his hand. 'When you mentioned Mossgate I put two and two together.'

He held her hand for longer than was necessary. His grasp was firm and warm. She resisted the urge to pull hers away, and forced herself to look into his face.

'I think you might have told me,' she said curtly.

'Might have told you what?'

'That you were a doctor. Leaving me in the dark like that—not really ethical, was it?'

Daphne was looking bemused. 'I take it you've met? Leigh, you said you didn't know Dr Christie.'

'I didn't think I did. I had met—for a few

minutes—someone called Adam who helped me with a resuscitation.' Leigh wasn't sure who had helped whom—a partnership, really. He seemed to read her thoughts.

'I thought we made an excellent partnership,' he said, his mouth twitching slightly. He *was* laughing at her! 'I take it we're to enjoy a professional relationship, Daphne?' he went on. 'My new health visitor, you said? What happened to the fat girl with the frizzy hair?'

'Maureen? Gone down with glandular fever. And Carol's not back until next April.'

'Ah, yes. Carol. Well, never mind. I'm sure Leigh—you did say Leigh, didn't you?—and I will make a splendid couple.'

Leigh knew what he meant, but for some reason the way he phrased it caused her cheeks to flame again. A splendid couple. The words that were used when two people decided to marry. And, for all she knew, she might have been right in her first impression of him as a nice family man. She could just see him with a brood of small children tagging after him. Yes, a girl about six, and a little blond boy like himself, and a toddler, perhaps another little girl, perhaps looking like her mother, like Mrs Christie . . . His wife. Small, dark, vivacious.

She herself wasn't that dark. Her hair was thick and a sort of nut-brown, and she kept it tied loosely back for work. Her eyes were hazel

18

with little gold flecks when the sun shone, and long, curling eyelashes. A boyfriend had once said her eyes were her best feature. He had been blond too. He'd said they looked good together. She couldn't remember his name.

Daphne was talking to her. 'You're staying with your mother, aren't you, Leigh?'

'Eh—sorry—yes. Banbury Road. Mrs Rochester.'

'I think I may have met her,' said Adam Christie, his gaze meeting hers. She pulled her thoughts away from wives and children, blonds and brunettes.

'I thought Dr Brent was her doctor?' she said.

'We're not always available for our own patients, as you put it. We are a group practice, after all. Sign on with one doctor, but you may have to see another. It's usual.'

'Yes, of course.'

'Well, I must be off, Daphne. Nice meeting you, Miss—' Adam emphasised the word '—Rochester. I'm sure we shall get on famously together.'

He gave her a quick smile and hurried down to the consulting-rooms with long, easy strides. Leigh watched him for a moment.

'Fancy it being him after all,' she murmured. But Daphne didn't reply. She was still gazing along the corridor, where Adam Christie had seemingly been buttonholed by a grey-haired man in a dark suit. She turned abruptly back to

19

Leigh.

'Did you say Stow-on-the-Wold?' she asked brightly.

'Stow? Oh—where I met Dr Christie. Yes—I'd stopped for a cup of coffee, and the man with the coronary—'

'That would explain it. That's where he comes from. That's where his family is—Stow.' Daphne turned towards the room they'd been about to enter. 'Have you met Graham yet? No, of course not—I got side-tracked. Come along, I'm starving.'

*　　*　　*

It was another fifteen minutes before Leigh's interview and tour was finally over. She'd met Graham Scott, a rather untidy man in his early sixties, in drooping beige cardigan and cavalry twill trousers, and momentarily she had been reminded of her father. Graham had shaken hands with her, wished her good luck, and gone back to his organisation of the bingo session. The prize was a bottle of wine.

She'd met two of the doctors: Arthur Brent, the man she'd seen talking to Adam Christie, rather brusque and serious, and Dr Thomas who was small and dark and vaguely Welsh. Daphne had finalised the arrangements for Leigh to start next Monday, and had passed a message to the chiropodist about Mrs Stokes's bunion.

'We don't wear a uniform,' Daphne had concluded, obviously itching to get at her lunch, 'so we don't get an allowance. Just look smart, that's all that matters. We're not keen on jeans.'

Leigh refrained from comment on Daphne's ancient twin-set, and held out her hand.

'I'm sure you'll fit in here,' Daphne said awkwardly. 'I only hope you don't go down with something.'

Leigh tidied herself in the staff cloakroom before leaving. She glanced at her watch as she crossed the car park. Quarter to two. Someone bumped into her.

'Oh—sorry—' she apologised.

'My fault, Miss Rochester; I didn't see you there.'

'That's all right, Dr Christie. No bones broken.' She looked up into his sky-blue eyes that seemed to be laughing at her. He always seemed to be laughing at her. What was so funny?

'I'd like a word with you, Dr Christie, if you can spare a moment,' she said.

'I think that could be managed. Would you care to come and have a cup of tea with me?'

'I'm trying to be serious.'

'So am I—very serious. But if you're too busy—'

'I wish you'd told me you were a doctor.'

'What difference would that have made? We saved the patient, didn't we, between us?

21

And, if it's any help, I rang the hospital and Mr Keith is holding his own, with every prospect of a good recovery.'

'That's gratifying to know, at least. But you should have told me. I felt such a fool just now, when you came striding along. In front of Daphne Horton too.'

He nodded. 'Yes, I can see how it could have been rather embarrassing for you. Please accept my apologies.'

'Very well. But you still haven't explained why you didn't tell me. What was so important about keeping it secret from me?'

He looked undecided. 'Do you want me to be honest?'

'Naturally.'

'You were doing so well, almost taking charge, as it were, and I didn't know you were a nurse either—' he gave her a reproachful glance '—and I figured if you were just a lay person who knew first aid—and knew it very well, I have to admit—I could have put you off your stroke by coming along and saying do it this way or that way, because I happen to be a doctor.'

Leigh didn't wait to see the logic in his statement. All she could think was—the conceit of the man! She stared at him, unable to speak for a moment. So he thought because he was a doctor he'd put her off her stroke, did he? Who did he think he was? She had never put doctors on pedestals, and she had no intention of starting now.

'You seem to have a very high opinion of doctors,' she finally said quietly, when she could speak without losing her temper.

'Not necessarily. I just know how people react towards us, and that includes most nurses, I have to admit. It isn't my fault if they put us on pedestals.'

Leigh couldn't hold it back this time. 'Well, here's one nurse who doesn't!' she blurted out. 'And I hope you realise it, or our professional relationship is not going to work!'

She wrenched at her car door and quickly sat down in her seat. She had said too much, she knew, but he had goaded her into it with his egotistical remarks. And now she'd ruined their relationship before it had even started.

No, she mustn't think like that, taking the blame for her reaction. But doctors and health visitors were partnerships, not master-and-slave relationships. She was not going down on her knees to him, if that was what he expected. Better to get that straight at the beginning.

She leaned out to close the door. Adam Christie was watching her quizzically, a professional look on his face. Oh, dear, now he was sizing her up from a psychological point of view.

'I'm sorry, Dr Christie, but I've wasted enough time already today, and I haven't had my lunch yet.'

'I'm sorry, too, that you think our meeting

23

was a waste of your time. I hope Mr Keith isn't included in that assessment. Good morning, Miss Rochester.'

She wanted to tell him it was now afternoon, but he was already striding across the car park to a gold-coloured BMW. Leigh sat and watched him. Damn, damn, damn! She'd really put her foot in it this time.

*   *   *

Leigh arrived at her mother's house in Banbury Road still feeling irritable and a little annoyed with Dr Christie. She'd been looking forward to working in her home patch after such a long time away. Was he going to spoil it all for her? She locked her car and marched up the path, fishing for her house keys in her bag, but before she could use them the front door had opened and her mother stood there. She was frowning—or was it just that her face had developed creases that way, as a consequence of her difficulties? She held the door with one hand, while the other rested heavily on a cane.

'So there you are, Leigh.' She leaned towards her daughter and kissed her on the cheek. 'I thought you'd be earlier than this. I've been watching out for you. I don't think Kate realises how lonely I get. But she insisted on getting that job, and I knew she'd find it awkward—'

'Kate got herself a job? I didn't know.'

Leigh followed her mother into the spacious square hall.

'In an estate agent's. Didn't I tell you? She was bored here all day with me. That explains why she isn't here to let you in. Hang your jacket up. That's a very smart suit, Leigh, but rather severe, don't you think?'

'I keep it strictly for special occasions, like interviews.'

Leigh hung her jacket in the cloakroom and followed her mother into the large, airy sitting-room. It seemed to be a little untidy, a bit dusty. Not as it usually looked. Did her mother leave everything to Kate? She wasn't a complete invalid.

'Kate said she needed the money,' Evelyn Rochester continued plaintively. 'I can't see why. She's never paid any rent here, and John gets a good salary. No, she was bored, but she wouldn't tell me to my face.' She sat down and looked at Leigh. 'It's going to be just lovely now you're back. You can't imagine how I've missed you. And, you being a nurse, you'll understand all my problems, won't you? Kate has never really understood. She's never tried, really. Been too busy with her own problems, I suppose.'

'Mother, I wish you wouldn't blame Kate like this. Of course she couldn't understand—she knows nothing about brain surgery. I wish she did, because then she wouldn't have given in to you so much. She's waited on you hand

and foot, and it was quite the wrong thing to do.'

'Leigh, how can you say such things? Are you suggesting she should have left me to do everything for myself? You know at the beginning I was almost totally helpless—'

'At the beginning, Mother. But it's ten years now. You should be—'

'Dr Williams said I'd always have a weakness in my leg and arm.'

'I know he did, and he's probably right. But Kate should have encouraged you to do a lot more than you have. If she had, then you might not even be using a stick now.'

Evelyn looked away. 'I didn't have the heart for it, not after . . .'

'After Dad died. Yes, I know. That shock didn't help. But I suppose it was easier for Kate to do things for you. Easier and quicker. And quite the wrong attitude to take,' Leigh finished.

'I didn't think you'd be coming back to bully me, Leigh.'

'I'm not bullying you, Mother. Although I may have to now and again.' Impulsively, she hugged her mother. 'I hate to see you like this, Mother. You're virtually a prisoner in your own home. I want to see you enjoying life, having fun again. You're still young, you may meet someone—'

Evelyn shook her head. 'There'll be no one else after Tom. There couldn't be anyone like

26

him.'

'How can you ever find out if you never go anywhere? Does Kate take you anywhere interesting?'

'They don't have much time. Anyway, I haven't the heart. People stare.'

'You imagine that, Mother. You're not the only one with a gammy leg. Kate should have made you go out with them. I can see now it's about time I did take over. Kate's had the difficult years—'

'You were only fifteen when it happened, Leigh. How could you have done anything? You were still at school.'

'I suppose I could have stayed at home instead of leaving to do my nursing training.'

'I wouldn't have heard of it, Leigh.' Her mother sounded indignant. 'Kate has never wanted a career. She was the best person to stay.'

'I wonder,' said Leigh softly. 'But perhaps it isn't too late. Perhaps we can still make something of your life.'

There was a wistful look in Evelyn's eyes as she murmured, 'If only . . .'

If only, Leigh echoed silently, thinking back to the days when she'd been a second-year student nurse here in Birmingham, at the Queen Anne. She had been on night duty on Kent Ward, and an emergency had arrived, a suspected brain abscess. The patient, a girl of seventeen, had attended the hospital

27

previously, so Leigh had been sent to collect her notes from the medical records office.

It was two a.m. and the records office had been dark and locked. Leigh had fetched the key from the porter's lodge, feeling rather nervous of the shadows that seemed to follow her, and the unexplained noises just around the next corner. She had hurried into the room, quickly turned on the light, and checked the card index for the number. Three-nine-two-four-four. She had run her fingers along the rows of beige, blue and green folders. Three-nine-two-four— She had grabbed at a folder—the wrong one. Three-nine-two-four-three. The name on it seemed to leap out at her: Evelyn May Rochester. Her mother. She had turned the covers, feeling guilty and excited. Well, why shouldn't she look? she had argued silently. It was her mother, wasn't it? She had a right to know. Instantly she had recalled the accident, five years before. They had said her mother had just stepped from the bus and walked straight in front of a lorry. Strange—her mother was always so very traffic-conscious. She wouldn't do a thing like that.

She'd been rushed into hospital with severe head injuries—a depressed fracture, they'd been told, pressing on the brain, causing bleeding. Kate had gone to pieces, but Leigh had remained cool, Leigh at fifteen had taken charge. They'd said then she'd make a good nurse. She smiled to herself as she remembered.

They'd operated. And afterwards they'd looked very serious, and told her and her father—who was fretting because he'd been in the middle of an important business deal—that they'd found something in Evelyn's brain when they'd looked inside, but they weren't to worry, it had been removed. It hadn't been malignant, but it had increased the risk during the operation. Because of its size she could be left with some residual damage.

At first, the whole left side of her body had been totally paralysed. As the months had passed, with continuous physiotherapy, some of this weakness had improved, and she'd begun to walk again and use her arm. Then, two years later, Mr Rochester had died suddenly.

Leigh put that memory aside, and concentrated on what the surgeon had said on the day of her mother's operation.

'A blessing in disguise. The tumour would have killed her within a few weeks. She's a very lucky woman.'

Evelyn had never looked at it that way. Then, when Tom died, she had sunk into apathy, stopped doing the exercises, refused to walk or use her hand. Leigh and Kate had worked really hard to get her through it, but she had never really recovered. And Leigh had never known why her mother had stepped

29

under the lorry. Had she felt giddy? It seemed likely. But there was no way of knowing, because Evelyn's memory of that time had gone completely. Months before the accident, months after it. Erased.

Leigh had turned the pages, glanced at the dates. The accident notes. The operation notes. The anaesthetic. Lots of long medical words, but she'd understood most of them— and the words of the casualty doctor, who had thought it likely Evelyn had lost her balance on stepping from the bus. Leigh had read quickly, so absorbed now that she'd almost forgotten it was two o'clock in the morning and she was all alone in the medical records office. The pre-med, the operation, the raising of the depressed fracture, the sealing of the injured blood vessels. And the discovery of the tumour, the size of a large walnut. Pressure on the eighth cranial nerve, arising from the meninges. A meningioma.

Leigh tried to remember it all, but it was so complicated. It had ended with a comment from the neurosurgeon.

It is hard to believe that this patient never presented herself to her doctor with symptoms of ataxia, giddiness, or headache. In my opinion this meningioma must have been causing disturbing and painful problems for some weeks at least.

30

Leigh had closed the folder. Her mind was churning. Her mother had been ill for weeks. Why didn't anyone know? Why hadn't she been referred to the hospital? Why hadn't she had tests? She must have spoken to someone. Why did they wait until she fell under a lorry?

She had pushed the notes back angrily, and had almost left the office when she'd remembered her real purpose for this visit. She'd flicked through the folders again, and found the correct one, then left the office and locked the door.

The staff nurse had frowned at her when she had returned. 'Where the hell have you been, Nurse Rochester? Mr Crane is here; he wants those notes. Come on; he's been dragged from his bed, and he's in a foul mood.'

She had snatched the folder from Leigh, who had protested weakly. She'd been too preoccupied to think up a reason for her lateness.

'They—they were misfiled. It took me ages to find them.' The staff nurse had glared at her, and told her to check the laryngectomy patient.

Leigh had never forgotten what she'd seen. And at her first opportunity she had gone to see her mother's doctor, Dr Williams.

'If only I could erase the last ten years.' Her mother was still musing aloud. 'Or at least remember why I wasn't seen earlier. You did say it wasn't my fault.'

'I don't think blaming anyone is going to help you now,' said Leigh gently. 'Although it would be nice for you if you could remember more of that time.'

Dr Williams's attitude had reinforced what she had concluded from the hospital notes. Her mother had seen someone, his locum. But Dr Williams had been quite angry, and had refused to discuss the matter with her. Understandable, she supposed. But it did make her think there was something he hadn't wanted her to know.

'I've tried so hard to remember,' said Evelyn, 'but it won't come. I just wish I could accept that I probably never shall.'

Leigh sighed.

She had grown to accept it herself, but it had taken time. It was still difficult when she watched her mother's dragging foot, her weak hand trying to hold things. Sometimes she gave up trying. Leigh knew it was up to her now to change this, to try to give back her mother her will and determination.

For the moment she decided to change the subject. 'Are you looking forward to joining Kate and John in Oxford soon?'

'I'm not so sure I want to leave here. I've lived here too long.'

Leigh looked at her mother. 'But who'll look after you if you stay?'

Evelyn's eyes widened. 'Isn't that why you

came back, Leigh? I thought that was why you'd changed your job?'

'It's only temporary, Mother—I thought I'd explained that. They expect me back in Bath next April. Carol will be back here by then.'

'Carol?'

'The girl I'm replacing here in Mossgate. She's on maternity leave.'

'And then you'll go back to Bath? What shall I do?'

'I thought that had all been arranged between you and Kate? Still, six months is a long time. I'm sure we can sort something out. For now, how about a cup of tea?'

'That would be nice, Leigh. I like one about now, but with Kate out all afternoon . . . And I find it difficult with only one good hand. I'm glad you'll be here to do it.'

Leigh paused by her mother's chair. 'I shan't be here to make it either, you know. I shall be working, except for weekends.'

'But your job's different, isn't it? You'll be able to call in whenever you want to, to see I'm all right. So convenient, really.'

Leigh sighed. 'Mother, you have the wrong idea about my job. Yes, I shall come home at lunchtime to help you, but otherwise I shall be very busy. I shall have calls to make, clinics to attend, doctors' meetings—' For no reason, her colour rose and she turned away awkwardly.

'You'll only be here at midday? How shall I

33

manage?'

'And mornings and evenings, and all night. Mother, I do want you to try to do more. I know you arm's still rather weak, but that's because you don't do the exercises Miss Pym left for you. Kate told me. And she didn't make you, either.'

'With the tennis ball, you mean? I think I've lost it.'

'Then I shall get you another. Oh, please, Mother! Please try!' Leigh hugged her mother. 'Look, why not come along to the Tuesday club at the health centre? You'd meet other people who are—who have mobility problems and such. I believe they have a lot of fun. I could take you and bring you home.'

'Oh, I couldn't, Leigh! What—and have everybody watching me? No, it's out of the question.'

'But they all have problems, Mother! They've had strokes and accidents and illnesses; they'd be just like you, probably worse. So why should they stare? And we have an exercise class on Fridays, and a physiotherapist, and an occupational therapist on Tuesdays. She could find a hobby for you to try.'

'I can't do hobbies with only one hand,' complained Evelyn. 'So stop making silly suggestions.'

'It's not a silly suggestion. There are people without hands who do hobbies. They paint with their feet, or their mouths.'

Evelyn stared at her for a moment as if unsure whether she was joking. Then she turned away, saying fretfully, 'I'm dying for that cup of tea.'

While they were relaxing over their tea Leigh told her mother how she had helped save a man's life earlier that day.

'It wasn't in hospital, it was in the street. A man had a heart attack.' She glanced at her mother, who had stopped drinking. 'I saved him. At least, with someone else. Gave him mouth-to-mouth and cardiac massage.'

'You really saved his life?' asked her mother quietly.

She nodded. 'We did. For the time being, anyway.'

'And he's still alive?'

'As far as I know.'

'An elderly man, was he?'

'Not really. Sixtyish, I suppose.' She swallowed. 'He looked a lot like Daddy. That's why I'm so glad we succeeded.'

'You keep saying "we". You had someone with you? It wasn't that librarian fellow, was it? Colin? Did he travel up with you?'

'No, Mother, I was alone. I stopped off at Stow-on-the-Wold for a cup of coffee, and found a nice little place. And there was this group of people, talking, and the man—the one who looked like Daddy—he just collapsed. I don't know where this—other fellow came from—' Leigh was reluctant to meet her mother's gaze in case her expression gave her away. Silly to let the man have this effect on her. He was, after all, arrogant and conceited and felt he should be worshipped. He'd said that much.

'Well, he was just there,' she went on. 'I did the breathing, he did the heart massage. Between us we got him going again. And they took him to hospital.'

There was a pause. Then Mrs Rochester said softly, 'He was lucky.'

'Yes, he was lucky, I suppose. Lucky we were there.'

'Luckier than Tom. Luckier than me, with this useless arm and leg—'

'Mother, you're not useless!' Leigh protested. 'You don't do your exercises any more, and Kate doesn't make you, and that's one of the reasons I'm coming home—to get you doing things.'

'Do you really think I could do more?' her mother asked softly, hopefully.

'I'm sure you could, Mother. And how will you ever know unless you try?'

'Sometimes I feel I'm just half a person. I drop things, and then I get despondent—'

Leigh drew her close, feeling a catch in her throat. 'Of course you do! That's to be expected. I'd feel the same. But that's all finished with. I'm back now, and I'm going to get you laughing, and going out, and enjoying

36

life again. And that's a promise!'

CHAPTER THREE

Leigh couldn't help releasing a sigh as she locked the front door of the house she shared with Dylis, one of the district nurses, and Margery, a schoolteacher at a nearby primary school. She'd been very happy there—they'd had lots of laughs, lots of fun at Margery's extrovert parties. She was going to miss it, going back to the quiet, staid life she'd had with her mother.

What am I thinking? she admonished herself, picking up her two heavy suitcases. I'm not leaving for good. I'm coming back in six months.

Am I? a little voice argued. And she recalled Miss Wainwright's words from this morning.

'You probably think I'm just being fanciful,' the senior health visitor had said, 'when I say I have a strong hunch you won't be coming back.'

A hunch? Down-to-earth Miss Wainwright with her sensible suits and flat shoes, her short, wiry grey hair and horn-rimmed spectacles? A hunch? People like her didn't have hunches. They stuck to the facts.

'It's just for maternity leave,' Leigh had

protested. 'Only six months.'

Miss Wainwright shrugged and smiled. 'I'd like to believe that. But I've had hunches before.' She didn't elaborate.

'I have no reason to stay there longer than six months,' Leigh persisted. 'My contract will end, and my mother will be going to live with my sister in Oxford. It's all planned.'

'Plans have a habit of going awry,' Miss Wainwright said darkly. 'Don't bank on it, that's all. Six months is a long time. Anything can happen.'

She fixed Leigh with a look of her shrewd grey eyes, and unaccountably Leigh suddenly had a vision of a tall young man with fair hair and eyes that always seemed to be laughing at her. Adam Christie. Embarrassed, she felt a flush start to creep into her cheeks. Miss Wainwright didn't appear to notice. She pushed some papers into a drawer.

'I'm very grateful you could stay to run the well baby clinic,' she went on, glancing at her watch. 'Perhaps you'd better get away now if you've got to travel to Birmingham this afternoon. I hope—' She looked embarrassed, and spoke gruffly. 'I hope you're very happy at Mossgate. I shall miss you.' She thrust out her hand.

Leigh was surprised to feel a lump in her throat as she took her hand for a moment.

'I'm coming back,' she said softly. Miss Wainwright gave her a little smile, and went

38

out to speak to the clinic doctor about a child.

As Leigh hurried down the stairs a few minutes later, her jacket over her shoulders, the doorbell rang. She sighed and glanced at her watch. The clinic had officially ended over half an hour ago, but there were always some parents who thought they could turn up whenever they felt like it, and still expected the staff to conjure up a doctor from thin air. Yet again, it could be a genuine emergency. If so, perhaps Miss Wainwright would deal with it. And the doctor hadn't yet gone.

She turned the heavy handle. 'I'm afraid the clinic—'

'Leigh. I hoped I wouldn't be too late.'

Leigh swallowed. She'd been afraid of this happening. 'I was just about to go, Colin. I have a long journey ahead of me, and the weather doesn't look too promising.'

'I won't keep you. I just came to say I hope you'll like it in Birmingham. And to ask you to keep in touch. You will keep in touch with me?'

His dark eyes looked intensely into her own, and she stifled a feeling of irritation. Heavens, he wasn't going to get all serious again, was he? And here on the doorstep of the clinic! Instinctively she glanced behind her at the empty hall.

'Of course I'll keep in touch, Colin. Now I really must go. I've still got some last-minute packing to do.'

'I'd come and help you, but we're short-staffed today. I had to grab this few minutes to come and see you off.'

'That was sweet of you, Colin.' Impulsively she kissed him lightly on the cheek. He grabbed her hand.

'I'm going to miss you awfully, Leigh.'

'It's only for six months. You can always give me a ring. You've got my address and number.'

She hoped he hadn't thought she was encouraging him. He was so nice, so kind, but he wasn't for her. She had felt rather guilty as she'd driven away, leaving him standing on the pavement, watching her. But perhaps it was for the best.

She put her suitcases on the damp pavement by her car and went back for her holdall. Half-past one, said Margery's hall clock. With a bit of luck she could do the journey in a couple of hours, but it was Friday, and there could easily be traffic jams. Say three hours to be on the safe side. Would she have time to stop off at Stow?

Now why did I think of Stow? she asked herself as she closed the boot lid on her luggage. She didn't have to stop at Stow. She could stop anywhere.

Well, I've found that nice little tea-shop in Stow, she argued with herself.

It's not that, the other little voice put in. It's because of Adam Christie.

Well, why should he be there today? He's

probably at Mossgate, working hard.

Leigh grimaced as she realised she'd been voicing her thoughts aloud. She hoped no one had heard her. They'd lock me up, she thought. And I'd never get to Mossgate.

She got in and fastened her seatbelt. There were dark clouds in the sky, and the wind was getting up.

*   *   *

She'd been right about the traffic. There was plenty of it. Twice she got caught in a long line of vehicles following a slow-moving caravan, and once it was a farm tractor doing about ten miles an hour.

He could have moved over to let us all pass, she thought frustratedly. But they never do. Eventually he turned into a farm entrance just outside Chippenham, and she tried to make up lost time. The sky was very dark now, and she wasn't keen on driving in heavy rain.

It was twenty-five past three as she approached Stow-on-the-Wold, and the first heavy spots of rain were falling. She thought longingly of the little tea-shop, Simpson's, with its cosy little tables, and the smell of coffee and cakes, and the hypnotic low hum of conversation. In response, her throat seemed to dehydrate, and the thought of a drink became overwhelming. Half-past three. Another hour would see her home. Yes. She turned off the Fosse Way and cruised along to the square. There seemed no place to park. Perhaps this wasn't such a good idea after all.

At the far end of the square, near the Cross, a white Ford was pulling out. Seeing the rain hitting her windscreen, Leigh didn't hesitate. As soon as the white car was free, she nipped in smartly, avoiding a red Fiat by just a few inches. Damn! She'd packed her umbrella in her suitcase. She'd just have to make a dash and hope for the best.

Pulling up the collar of her jacket, she shoved her bag under her arm and, head down, hurried along Digbeth towards the tea-shop. Raindrops were hitting her head with some force. Why hadn't she thought to put a couple of cans of Coke or something in her car? Because she'd rushed, that was why, with visions of Colin turning up again to help her pack. She hadn't wanted to prolong the agony of their separation—Colin's agony, not her own.

The pavements were shiny with rain. Out of the corner of her eye she saw a clock-shop as she passed. She'd toyed with the idea of buying Kate and John a clock for Christmas. But this was an antique shop, and the clocks were way out of her price range.

She turned quickly away from the tempting display in the windows. Perhaps one day she'd come back here, take a longer look. A tall figure suddenly materialised in front of her, too suddenly for her to change direction. They met with a soft thud, her bent head firmly against his chest. *His* chest. A man. She looked up.

'I'm sorry— You!'

'You!'

They spoke simultaneously. Colour rushed to Leigh's face.

'We appear to be making a habit of this.' Adam Christie's voice seemed to be teasing. She tried not to look into his bright blue eyes.

'Yes, we do. Quite a coincidence, meeting you here again.' Her words sounded stilted and awkward. She felt awkward.

'Not really. I live here—now and again, that is. I take it you're on your way to Birmingham again?'

'I am.'

'Well—aren't you going in the wrong direction?' He was laughing at her! She lifted her chin defiantly. Her hazel eyes glittered.

'Will you leave the direction to me, Dr Christie? I do know where I'm going.'

His mouth quivered slightly. 'It's a long way to walk, you know. What time were you planning to arrive? And aren't you going to get rather wet?'

'I'm getting very wet standing here talking to you! If you don't mind—' She gave him an exasperated look. A raindrop fell from her hair on to her nose, and she wiped it away.

'Simpson's?' Adam suggested.

'That's just where I was going when you walked into me.'

'I? Oh—never mind. That explains the direction,' he agreed, taking her arm. Instinctively, she began to withdraw it, but it felt cosy and companionable, so she left it there. He was wearing a green waterproof anorak with the hood pulled up, and a lock of damp blond hair straggled on to his forehead. She had to hurry to keep up with his long strides, but within seconds they were at the tea-shop, and safely inside.

'Tea or coffee?' asked Adam, as Leigh tried to tidy her thick, damp hair.

'Oh—please—let me—' she began.

'Not at all. This is my town, so my treat. How about that little table by the window?'

Before Leigh could agree—or even disagree—she was seated opposite him at the small table, and he was giving his order.

'Toasted tea-cakes, Leigh?' He smiled at the waitress. 'Tea-cakes for two.' He turned to Leigh. 'So you've been in here before.'

'Yes, the day Mr Keith had his—that's why—'

'Of course! I did wonder at the time what you were doing in Stow when you were on your way to Birmingham, but naturally I was more concerned that Mr Keith was parcelled off to hospital quickly.'

'Naturally. Do you know how he is?' Leigh asked.

'Coming along well, I believe. His wife said she'd be in touch with you.'

'There's really no need. I was only doing my job.'

'Now you're all prickly again. I wonder why?'

'I'm not—' She broke off as the tea and toasted tea-cakes arrived, the butter melting over the golden-brown surfaces. She bit into one, and the butter squelched out and trickled down her chin. She grabbed at the paper napkin to wipe it away.

'This is really delicious, Dr Christie, but there really was no need to—'

'What's all this "Dr Christie" business? Are you always so formal with your friends?'

'I thought we were colleagues,' she said.

'And is there any reason why colleagues can't also be friends?'

'It's not—professional, is it?'

He put on an expression of mock severity. 'I can see you were brought up in the old school. Business and pleasure don't mix. Am I right?'

'That's what my father always said,' she told him.

'Said? Has he changed his mind now?'

'He died.'

'I'm sorry.' He looked up at her. 'From business or pleasure?'

'A heart attack. And I'd really rather not talk about it, if you don't mind.' She took a mouthful of tea.

Adam Christie surveyed her for a moment before biting into his tea-cake. 'You'd prefer me to call you Miss Rochester, then?'

'I don't really mind.'

He nodded. 'Then I shall call you Leigh. My name's Adam, or did I already tell you?'

'You did.'

There was another awkward pause. Despite the delicious tea-cake, Leigh was beginning to have doubts about stopping off in Stow. What was it about Adam Christie that made her hackles rise? Was it his constant good humour, his perpetually laughing eyes? Or just her own sensitivity that he might be laughing at her? Did he really find life such a joke?

She recalled the way he'd dealt with Mr Keith the other day, his skill, his professionalism. She should have guessed then that he'd had some medical training. Perhaps he'd believed it to be obvious, and that was why he hadn't told her. He'd probably been amused that she hadn't guessed.

Now look what I'm doing, she argued silently. I'm making excuses for him!

'Penny for them. Or are they worth more in these days of inflation?'

Leigh started, and turned to find him gazing at her. She'd been wrong; his blue eyes weren't always laughing. They were watching her with a strange sort of speculation in them, and something else she couldn't quite analyse. She felt herself flushing. 'I was just—thinking

46

about someone.'

'Ah!'

'It's not who you think,' she said defensively.

'And who do I think it may be? Let's see. Your father? Possibly—you changed the subject rather quickly there. Perhaps we ought to discover why. Not your father, then. Your mother? Not much point, since you'll soon be seeing her. Unless you're worried about her. No? Your boyfriend? That's a strong possibility. Could be the reason you're so prickly with me. You've left him behind, and you're worried he might find someone else.'

'No—it's not like that at all!' she burst out, and immediately regretted it. Adam raised his eyebrows.

'Not the boyfriend, then. Ah, well, there can only be one other person.' He smiled, showing a dimple in his cheek.

'And who might that be?'

'Yours truly. I—myself—me.'

Because he had guessed so accurately, Leigh felt her cheeks grow red with embarrassment.

'Really!' she blustered. 'You've never heard of modesty, have you? Why should I be thinking about you, when you're sitting opposite me?'

'All the more reason. And that could be why you're so prickly. You've fallen head over heels in love with me!'

And now his eyes *were* laughing at her.

Leigh put down her cup and wiped her mouth. She was fighting for control.

'I don't think I've ever heard such conceit in all my life!' She jumped up and grabbed her bag. 'And I've got better things to do with my time than sit here listening to such arrogance! I'll pay for my own tea, thank you. You might misconstrue my willingness to let you pay!'

She put her purse down on the table, but Adam Christie's hand quickly closed over hers.

'Leigh, where's your sense of humour?'

He leaned forward, and his face was only inches from her own. His eyes were very, very blue, and serious now. His full lips tilted at the corners. They were really quite kissable. She felt her pulses suddenly starting to race. This would never do!

'Oh, I see,' she said. 'It was meant to be funny.'

'Well, naturally. Surely you didn't think I was really suggesting you'd fallen in love with me?'

She couldn't answer; she knew she'd say the wrong thing. His eyes widened.

'You did! Oh, Leigh, I'm sorry—'

She pulled her hand free, and picked up her purse. 'It doesn't matter.' She realised she'd made an utter fool of herself. She should have gone along with his suggestion, agreed she was madly in love with him. Made a joke of it, as he'd expected. She'd displayed quite the wrong reaction, and now he would think her prim and dreary and not worth knowing. Suddenly she didn't want him to think of her like that. She gave a wobbly smile.

Adam took her arm. 'Why don't we forget all that silliness I said, and start again?' he suggested.

Leigh hesitated. This was her opportunity to make things right between them. They would be working together, after all. Disliking him at this early stage wouldn't help their professional relationship. Six months was a long time.

She sat down again. 'As long as you promise not to laugh at me all the time.'

He adopted a mock-severe expression. 'I shan't smile at all in your presence,' he promised, his blue eyes refusing to stop twinkling. Against her will, Leigh burst out laughing.

'That's much better,' said Adam.

CHAPTER FOUR

'So Kim will be going to school soon, Mrs Fletcher,' said Leigh, sipping the milky coffee the woman had given her. Susan Fletcher tucked a strand of long blonde hair behind her ear. She habitually wore a strained, anxious expression on her thin face, and her fingers plucked constantly at her cardigan. Leigh wondered if she had something on her mind.

'Oh, no, not until next September. She missed this year's entry by six days. And they don't take them after Christmas and Easter any more, the way they used to. It's such a shame. Her little friend's birthday was in August, so she could start, and Kim was really upset about it, being left behind. I do think they ought to take them at Christmas and Easter, don't you?'

Leigh smiled and nodded as the woman rambled on. She didn't interrupt. Sometimes it helped them just to be able to talk; sometimes they said more than they'd intended, revealed hidden worries and fears. She put down her cup.

'That was a lovely cup of coffee, Mrs Fletcher. And I'm glad to hear Kim's eating better after that bad dose of gastroenteritis.'

'It was a good thing, in a way. She was getting ever so finicky, just before, and my mother used to say—' Mrs Fletcher paused, and tugged at a button on her cardigan. 'Well, I was very finicky as a child.' She gave Leigh a falsely bright smile.

'Does your mother live near enough to help you with the children, Mrs Fletcher?'

Susan Fletcher's face clouded over again. The line between her brows reappeared.

'She's dead, Miss— She died when I was a teenager. And I didn't marry until I was thirty, so my children just have the one grandmother, and she lives in Surrey, so they don't see much of her.' She tugged again at the button, and it came off in her hand. She tutted. 'I was seventeen when my mother died. I had to look after my two younger brothers.' She jumped up and removed the empty cup from Leigh's hand. 'More coffee? Did you say your name was Rochester? As in *Jane Eyre*?'

'That's right,' Leigh smiled. 'No relation. No, I won't have another one, thank you.'

'Will you be coming again?'

'Not for some time. As Kim is four, I don't need to see her as often as I see the little ones. Unless—did you particularly want me to come again? Is something wrong?'

'Oh, no, not really. I shouldn't take up so much of your time. It's a medical problem, really. I'll go and see Dr Christie. He's so nice, and always listens.'

'Aren't you well?'

'Just headaches, that's all—rather a lot of headaches. Stress, I suppose. I don't expect it's anything serious.' Mrs Fletcher was watching for Leigh's reaction.

'Do you think it might be something serious? Such as?'

'Well, I did think it might be high blood-pressure, something like that. But I expect I'm just making a fuss. Now I must let you go, or you'll never get all your visits done. I do admire you medical people; you have such difficult jobs, but so busy all the time. It's nice to be busy. Takes your mind off things. I'm sorry Kim wasn't here to see you, but she loves her nursery school . . .' Mrs Fletcher smiled apologetically.

'Mrs Fletcher, if you really think you have something wrong, you must go and see Dr Christie, or Dr Powell,' Leigh told her. 'You mustn't sit and worry about it.'

'I'll go next week. I promise.' She followed Leigh to the door, and waved energetically as she drove away.

High blood-pressure, thought Leigh, as she drove along Hillwood Avenue towards the health centre. She was a bit young for it. Probably just stress. But she's worried about something. I'll find some excuse to call on her again in a couple of weeks, she promised herself.

*   *   *

She had just left her office to go home for lunch when Adam Christie buttonholed her.

'Glad I've found you, Leigh,' he said, without preamble. 'I've got a lady I want you to see.'

His grasp of her arm was firm. She turned to face him, her clear hazel eyes meeting his bright blue ones. Not much like an October sky, she couldn't help thinking. Always summer with Adam Christie around. And her thoughts made her flush. What a good job he

52

couldn't know what she was thinking!

'Who is she?' she asked.

'Mrs Varley, Mouse Lane. Shall we discuss it in here?' They went into the vacant health visitors' office that Leigh had just left. He perched on the edge of Pauline's untidy desk, Leigh stood against the filing cabinet. He swivelled round to look at her.

'I haven't met Mrs Varley yet,' she said. 'Tell me about her.'

'Of course. It's early days yet, but you seem to have made your mark. Mrs Jesson has actually changed her mind about having Christopher immunised. I've been trying to persuade her for weeks.'

'Combined effort, I suppose,' said Leigh, and self-consciously adjusted the black velvet bow that held her heavy nut-brown hair at the nape of her neck.

'Mrs Varley,' said Adam, 'is in her early forties. She married about eight years ago, for the second time. Her first marriage, when she was a teenager, produced a baby boy who, unfortunately, died suddenly for no apparent reason at the age of seven months. A cot death, I presume—sudden infant death syndrome.'

Leigh resisted the urge to tell him she did know the correct title. 'Tragic,' she murmured.

'Very. She divorced her husband—I think he always blamed her for the cot death—'

'Oh, that was cruel!'

53

'As you said once, when you can't face up to the truth, it's very easy to blame someone. She didn't marry again until she was in her early thirties, a nice, mature man who idolises her, but makes no bones about the fact that he wants a family.'

'She still feels guilty about the first baby, I suppose,' said Leigh.

'I don't know.' He looked at her. 'You'll have to ask her. I think part of her problem is psychological, and may well be the result of that event. She may tell you if you ask her.'

'So what's her problem now? She can't conceive? Could it be the husband?'

'She did conceive, after a number of years, but she miscarried at eight weeks. It didn't seem to have a terrible effect on her—not apparent, anyway. In June she conceived again, and in early September she miscarried. I've talked to her, suggested she go to the hospital to see if she has some fault in her cervix. But she's very resistant, seems to have grown fatalistic about the whole thing. I'm dreadfully afraid she's suppressing it all.'

'Does she want to be pregnant?' asked Leigh astutely.

'You've hit the nail on the head. I want you to go and talk to her, woman to woman. Ferret out the guilt which I'm sure is there. Can you do it?'

'I can but try,' she said.

'If I had more time I'd try to counsel her,

but that seems to be the commodity I just don't seem to have much of. I've touched on the subject, but she just shrugs her shoulders, says, "What's the point?"'

Leigh's eyes darkened with sympathy. 'She's hurting.'

Adam stepped down from his perch and stood close to her. Too close . . .

'I'm sure you're right, Leigh. She's hurting. As usual, your diagnosis is spot-on. Leigh—I'm glad you came.'

She couldn't step backwards—she was already against the filing cabinet. She tried to appear unconcerned by his proximity, but her heart was thumping.

'Well, I'm glad too. And I shall certainly do my best for Mrs Varley.' She moved quickly sideways and went across to her own desk, where she fiddled about among the papers. Adam watched her for a moment.

'I shall be here until about five o'clock if you do manage to see her today. Did I say she lives in Mouse Lane? I've got her notes if you need to refer to them. I don't expect you have a file on her, since she doesn't have children. She's number 26, the top end, near Shakespeare Way.'

Leigh nodded, still not looking at him. She pretended to be absorbed in the papers, and a few seconds later he left. She sat down, sighing.

Mouse Lane led off the main Oxford road, a quiet, tree-lined avenue of pre-war semi-detached houses. There were no children playing nor dogs barking when Leigh drew up outside number 26. Just a couple of women chatting on the pavement, who glanced curiously at her as she pushed open the small wrought-iron gate and walked up the path.

Pamela Varley was a short, plump woman with rather lank, dark hair, wearing a food-spotted yellow sweater over crumpled brown trousers. Leigh didn't know why, but the word depression came into her mind.

Pamela gave her a bright smile when Leigh introduced herself.

'A health visitor? I thought you just visited families with children.' She closed the front door behind them. The house smelled vaguely unclean.

'Well—' began Leigh.

'Because I don't have any children. Didn't they tell you, whoever sent you? I was pregnant, but it died.'

Leigh stared at her. It died? A slip of the tongue?

'Died?' she said slowly. 'I thought—'

'A miscarriage—I meant I had a miscarriage. Come on in here. It's a bit untidy, but I got up late.'

'A miscarriage—I'm sorry. You must be

56

upset,' said Leigh.

'Died, miscarriage—it's all the same thing, isn't it?' Pamela Varley spoke over-brightly, perching on the arm of the sofa. Leigh sat down carefully next to some unfinished knitted. Pale lemon knitting.

'It isn't the same thing at all, Pamela—may I call you Pamela? You didn't have a miscarriage because it died. There is a difference.'

Pamela frowned and fiddled with her hair. It needed washing. Leigh decided it was time to change the subject. She smiled at her.

'Cup of tea?' asked Pamela Varley.

'I'd love one. Thank you.'

Pamela clattered about noisily in the small kitchen, while Leigh gazed about her. It was a through-lounge, the dining-room and sitting-room made into one, and in the rear garden a white shirt hung damply from a clothes-line; almost stationary in the still October day.

It won't dry, she thought. There's no wind. And no sun in this house either.

Pamela offered her biscuits from an opened packet. Leigh refused, but accepted the mug of weak tea. Pamela sat opposite, cradling her mug in her hands.

'So who sent you?' she asked. 'You couldn't have known about me unless someone had told you.'

'No,' Leigh admitted. 'It was Dr Christie. He was concerned about you.'

'I can't think why. I'm perfectly all right, as you can see. I'm actually a very busy person, no time for a baby, really, so perhaps it's a good thing. I go to lots of classes at the local institute—cookery, painting and sketching—but I'm not much good, and I've made lots of friends, and we meet on Fridays for coffee—'

Yes, thought Leigh. You make yourself busy so you don't have time to think. She smiled and nodded.

'Yes, and this year I've started two O levels because I missed out on them the first time round—too busy enjoying myself, and then, of course, I got a bit tied up—' Pamela's mouth twisted wryly. Leigh seized her opportunity.

'Ah, yes, you married very young, didn't you?'

'You can say that again! I couldn't have been any younger.'

'You mean you were only sixteen?' Leigh sipped her tea. It was too milky and had sugar in it.

'Just sixteen. Well, I had to, didn't I?' Pamela stared defiantly at Leigh, who gave her an encouraging smile.

'You were pregnant.'

'I suppose you're going to preach at me now, aren't you? Pregnant at fifteen.'

'Mrs Varley—Pamela—I'm not here to judge anyone. I'm here to help.'

'Well, I don't need any help. Can't you see that?'

58

'Tell me more about that time. When you were sixteen.'

'You won't believe this, but I was in love with the guy—Steve, his name was. All my friends were in love with him, but I got him. What a way to get someone, trapping them with a baby! That's what he said, anyway.'

'He blamed you?' asked Leigh.

'Blamed me for everything. For the baby—for everything.'

'Everything? You mean—when the baby died too?'

Pamela cast her a quick glance. 'You know about that, do you? Well, of course, Dr Christie will have told you. Yes, he blamed me for that too.' She gulped at her tea and took a bite of digestive biscuit. 'Everyone blames me for everything. I'm used to it.'

I was right about the depression, thought Leigh. I'll have to do something.

'The miscarriages too? But they can't be your fault.'

'Try telling Carl. Oh, he hasn't said as much, but he thinks it, I can tell.'

'Oh, Pamela, I'm sure that's not true!' Leigh protested.

'You think I'm imagining it? That's what they all say.' Pamela leaned forward. 'When you live with someone, you know.'

'Your husband wants a family, doesn't he? I expect he's disappointed.'

'And what about me? Aren't I

59

disappointed?'

More than that, thought Leigh. You're in agony.

'Pamela, why are you letting them all blame you?' she asked gently.

Pamela seemed taken aback. 'Letting them? What—what do you mean?'

'I get the impression you expect them to blame you. Almost as if you feel you deserve to be blamed.'

Pamela's eyes widened. Her knuckles were white round the mug of tea. 'You're blaming me too!' she whispered, tears forming in the corners of her eyes.

'No,' said Leigh gently. 'You're blaming yourself. I'm blaming no one. What happened to your last two babies was no one's fault—in as much as your body may have rejected them, for psychological reasons.'

Pamela didn't seem able to answer. She stared at Leigh, the pupils of her eyes huge with shock.

'And what happened to your first baby was no one's fault. Despite what Steve said, it wasn't your fault.'

Pamela licked her lips. 'But you don't know,' she said hoarsely. 'You don't know what happened! It *was* my fault!'

Leigh hid her surprise. Not such a surprise, really. Most mothers of babies dying from SIDS blamed themselves for some sin of omission or commission.

'Tell me what happened, Pamela.' She put down her half-drunk tea.

'I was just seventeen.' Pamela's voice was almost inaudible. 'Matthew had been crying all morning—screaming. He must have been teething. I got furious with him. He wouldn't take his two o'clock feed, so I put him in his cot and went downstairs. He was still crying, but I knew he was tired.

'I'd got a good book from the library, so I went downstairs and read for a while. He must have dropped off, and then I fell asleep on the sofa. I didn't wake up until nearly five o'clock. I thought I heard Matthew upstairs—a little noise, but he wasn't crying, so I left him alone. I didn't want to start him off again because I'd got to get Steve's tea on.'

Pamela paused, took another gulp of tea. Leigh didn't say anything, just smiled encouragingly.

'The meal was in the oven, and Steve hadn't come home, so I went up to see to Matthew. I felt guilty because I'd been so angry with him, and anyway, it was almost time for his six o'clock feed.' She shuddered slightly, and Leigh tensed. 'He was just lying there, icy cold. I could see—'

'Icy cold?' echoed Leigh.

'If only I'd gone up at five when I heard him—'

'Mrs Varley—Pamela—you couldn't have heard him at five o'clock,' Leigh said.

'Yes—I heard something—'

'Not the baby. If he was icy cold when you went in at six, he must have been dead for quite a time—since he first fell asleep. You couldn't have known, and it wasn't your fault.'

Pamela swallowed. 'But I heard— He was already dead?'

'He must have been, if he was so cold. Was the room cold?'

'Not really. It was part of a house that we shared with an old lady, and it was centrally heated. Anyway, it was summer—July. A hot day.'

'Pamela, I'm absolutely certain the baby's death wasn't your fault. Why did you let your husband blame you?'

Pamela looked away. 'Because I'd never wanted Matthew. I hated being pregnant. I felt he was intruding on my life, I wanted a good time, parties, dances, fun.' She looked up. 'Don't get me wrong. Once I'd got him, I loved him. I think I loved him too much. Trying to make up for my rejection of him, I suppose. I really did love him!'

Tears cascaded down her face. Leigh held her shaking shoulders until her sobs subsided.

'Of course you loved him. I suppose you didn't tell anyone what you've just told me—about falling asleep, hearing a noise at five?'

Pamela shook her head dumbly. She pulled a tissue from a box and blew her nose noisily.

'It made no difference. Steve still blamed

me. We separated a year later. I thought I'd have all my fun then, but I had no heart for it. I couldn't stop thinking about Matthew.' She gave a wry smile. 'All these years—'

'You must forget it all now,' Leigh told her. 'Forget all that guilt. You can have a baby— Good God, Pamela, you deserve a baby after all that!'

*   *   *

Leigh returned to the clinic at four-thirty, to write up her visits. She also made a mental note to see Adam Christie about Pamela Varley.

Daphne Horton was still at the maternity hospital, after giving a talk and demonstration to antenatal mothers. Leigh wrote quickly. At twenty to five Pauline Morris hurtled in, rummaged among the papers on her desk, opened and shut drawers, and swore softly to herself.

'Have you lost something?' asked Leigh.

'It was here this morning—I saw it when I was writing that report on the family in the battered wives' hostel. It must be here—' She scrabbled furiously.

'Important?' asked Leigh.

'I promised Mrs Cleaver. She wants a registered child-minder, and I've got the list somewhere. I know it should be kept on the board, but I—oh, here it is; I'll pop it in to her before I go home. See you, Leigh.' She paused at the door. 'Getting on all right?'

'Yes, thanks. I'm fine.' Except when Dr Christie steps on my toes.

'Get on with Ol' Blue-Eyes, do you?'

'Sorry? Who? Oh—'

'Adam Christie. Lucky you. But he's a confirmed bachelor. You knew that? Didn't Daph tell you? Yes, some sad love-affair in his youth. He can't forget her. Still, don't let that stop you. You're pretty, you're slim.'

'Pauline, I'm sure he's not the slightest bit interested in my face or my figure. And I hope he's not, too. He's got more important things on his mind, and so have I.'

So why did the merest mention of the man's name bring his face to her mind, with those sky-blue eyes and those kissable lips? Kissable lips? What on earth was she thinking about?

'And so have I!' said Pauline, pulling the door open. 'Got to get this list to Mrs Cleaver. Still, best of luck with Dr Christie— Oh, sorry!'

Blushing like a beetroot, she squeezed past the figure who had just materialised in the doorway, and scurried down the corridor.

Adam Christie stood for a moment watching her, a smile creasing his features. Then he turned to Leigh, who was feeling as embarrassed as Pauline. Surely Adam would think they had been discussing him! Best of luck with Dr Christie, Pauline had said, and he must have heard it. What would he think of her?

She lowered her head and pretended to be busily writing in her register. He came over to her desk and perched on the edge. His thighs were muscular under his grey trousers. She closed the book with a flourish and stood up. Now she was more or less on his level.

'I visited Mrs Varley,' she said, trying to keep her gaze from his sensual mouth. 'I was just writing about it, before coming to see you. I take it that's why you're here?'

'Mrs Varley? Oh, yes, of course. Naturally I'm concerned about her. How is she?'

'For a start, she's very depressed. At least, she seemed depressed when I arrived.'

'And you wrought some miracle cure? That's marvellous! Just think what it will mean. No more tricyclics or MAO inhibitors, no more lithium, et cetera. Just call Leigh Rochester, and she'll achieve a cure in one visit.' His mouth twitched.

'I wish you'd stop laughing at me! No, I don't suppose I did wreak any miracle cure, but she did tell me a lot about the first baby, and you were quite right, she was full of guilt. And I don't suppose one visit will have eradicated all that guilt, so I'm going back next week. But she was certainly improved—'

'It wasn't I who suggested she was full of guilt,' said Adam. 'If I remember correctly, you suggested that, and I agreed. So it

65

seems you're an expert diagnostician, Leigh Rochester. Perhaps you should have been a doctor, or a psychiatrist.'

She flushed. She knew he didn't mean it. 'Now you're being sarcastic again.'

His eyes widened. 'Indeed I am not. I'm being most sincere. But I have to admit an ulterior motive. I've also come to ask a favour of you.'

'Someone else you want me to see? Can't it wait until tomorrow?' She was suddenly aware that her face was level with his and that he seemed to have moved fractionally closer. She sat down again.

'Oh, no, this can't wait. This is very important. Have you ever heard of the Mossgate Players?'

'Of course I have—I lived here for eighteen years. In fact, if I hadn't moved out to take up nursing, I might even have joined them.'

'You've done amateur dramatics?' He sounded excited.

'Only at school. But I enjoyed it. And I think everyone should have a hobby. I'm not much good at anything else.'

'Have you seen any of their plays?' he asked.

'I went with Kate and Mother a couple of times. We thought it would do Mother good, but it was rather too soon after her operation, and she found the sitting uncomfortable. We saw *Blithe Spirit*. And *The Winslow Boy*, I think it was. They were very good.'

He was still watching her, and she suddenly suspected that he was asking her out! She felt her pulses begin to race.

'If we're going to see them, you'd better tell me what they're putting on,' she said. 'It sounds like fun. I haven't been to see a play for ages.'

She was amazed when he laughed out loud. 'I wasn't asking you to see a play with me. I was asking you to join in!'

'Join in? I don't understand.'

'I'm a member of the Mossgate Players—we're putting on a play in the New Year. We rehearse on Thursdays, and that's why I had to see you now, before you go home. When you said you'd acted before, I just knew you were the right person.'

'You want me to be in your play? Why?' asked Leigh.

'I'll be honest. One of the girls has broken her leg, so we need another Amanda in a hurry. I immediately thought of you.'

'But Adam, I couldn't! There's my mother—I couldn't leave her—'

'You just said it sounded like fun. You agreed to come.'

'I misunderstood. I thought it was for just one evening, not every week.'

Yes, I thought you were offering to take me out, when in reality you were just using me, she thought.

67

'Surely you could have one evening a week out? She's not such a tartar, is she?'

'She's not a tartar at all. But she depends on me.'

'If I recall correctly, she isn't totally dependent on you. She can do things for herself. Are you sure you're not just making excuses?'

'No—but you took me rather by surprise—'

'Then say you'll do it! I was banking on your saying yes.' Adam put on a sheepish expression. 'I told Roger you would.'

'Who's Roger? You had no right to make decisions for me!'

'Roger's the producer. I didn't mean to spring it on you like this, but he only rang me this morning, to tell me about Julie's accident. He couldn't think of anyone of the right sort of age. I said—'

'I really have to think about it, Adam. Let me—'

'There isn't time—the rehearsal is tonight. And I'm sure you'd be a perfect Amanda.'

Leigh left her desk and walked across to the window. The scarlet berries of the rowan tree lay sprinkled over the damp grass. A watery sun was trying to break between the clouds. She felt confused. Part of her wanted to fall in with Adam's plans; part of her was warning her not to get involved. She seemed to sense a strange sort of premonition that this was going to prove a significant turning-point in her life.

And it all depended on whether she said yes or no.

Behind her, she heard Adam lever himself off the desk and walk softly towards her. She made up her mind quickly, and turned to face him. He seemed to give off a sort of animal magnetism, an electric current that drew her towards him. She looked up at him. 'I'll do it. But only on condition I can drop out—tonight—if I don't like it. I hope it's not a large role?'

'Oh, no. The big part is Celia, my faithful but rather drab fiancée. Amanda's supposed to be a siren, trying to lure me away.'

'Does she succeed?' Why did she suddenly feel she had to know this? Was it because she felt a pang of jealousy towards the unknown girl who took the part of Celia?

'Oh, no, Celia gets wise to her. Don't worry, you'll get a copy of the play to read at leisure. Now, I'll I pick you up at your house at seven o'clock? You'll feel more at ease if you arrive with me.'

Leigh doubted this, but she knew what he meant. 'You know where I live?'

'Corner of Banbury Road and Rose Hill. I have a patient next door. Don't be late.' He turned to go.

'Adam—' He looked at her, 'Adam, do you really think I can play the part of a siren?'

He laughed. 'All women can.' At the door he looked back. 'Thanks.'

Leigh sat at her desk. It was really nothing of importance, just taking part in an amateur play. So why did she feel so uneasy?

*   *   *

'Do you think trousers are suitable, Leigh?' asked Evelyn Rochester, as Leigh came downstairs in her chocolate-brown cords, and a primrose-yellow sweater. Her thick hair hung loosely on her shoulders. The sweater seemed to pick up the gold in her hazel eyes, which sparkled excitedly. She'd done her best to hide the apprehension she felt. She had put on more make-up than she wore for work, and a little blusher on her cheeks.

'Believe me, Mother, trousers will be ideal for what I'm going to do. I remember the school plays, climbing everywhere!'

'You look so boyish in trousers,' said Evelyn. 'Wouldn't a loose frock be comfortable? Men like to see girls in frocks.'

'Mother, I'm joining this drama group because they need someone quickly, not to attract a man.'

'Pity. You're not getting any younger. Look at Kate, married at eighteen, a baby the next year. I'd like more grandchildren, Leigh.'

'Well, I have no intention of grabbing the first man who comes along, just to satisfy your grandmotherly urges. I expect I shall get married eventually, but I'm not rushing things.

I enjoy my career,' Leigh said.

Her mother gave her a sidelong glance. 'What happened to that nice librarian you talked about? Have you fallen out?'

'Colin? No, Mother, we haven't fallen out. But we're really just good friends, that's all.'

'That's what they all say.'

Just then the doorbell rang, and Leigh hurried to open it. Adam seemed taller than ever, in jeans, checked shirt, and denim jacket. She was glad about her trousers.

'It's Adam,' she called back to her mother. 'Do you need anything?'

'I can't find my library book. And the *Radio Times*. Will you look for me, Leigh?'

'You'd better come in for a moment, Adam,' said Leigh. 'Mother won't rest until I've found them.'

He followed her into the hall, glancing at a painting with interest. Evelyn appeared at the door of the kitchen, and stared at him for a moment.

'Dr Christie,' she said slowly, looking puzzled.

'Hello, Mrs Rochester. How are you?'

She shrugged and didn't answer. She turned to Leigh.

'Is the kettle ready for my drink?' she asked. Leigh followed her into the kitchen. She was frowning.

'What is it, Mother? What are you trying to do? You know it's all ready—you watched me do it.'

'It's Dr Christie. Leigh, I think my memory's coming back!'

Leigh stared at her. 'But you already know Dr Christie. He's been to see you once or twice. But that was recently—he told me.'

'Yes, I know. And I've just realised I've seen him before, a long time ago. He was a doctor at the hospital when I had my operation. It's true, Leigh—my memory's coming back!'

CHAPTER FIVE

Evelyn's eyes shone. She looked younger and happier. At first Leigh didn't understand what she was trying to say.

'Dr Christie looked after you when you were in hospital—ten years ago?' she questioned.

'Yes, isn't it marvellous? I remember his face quite clearly. I can't think why I didn't when he came to see me in the spring—you remember, Leigh, when I had that awful bronchitis. And when I had that allergy—well, I always said it was an allergy—he thought it was nerves. No, it was just now, seeing him standing there in the hall. Oh, Leigh, if my memory's coming back, perhaps all the use will come back in my arm and leg! Perhaps I shall get back to normal!'

'Mother, that's great, it really is. But don't

raise your hopes too much. Ten years is a long time. It's not usual for a sudden recovery to happen after that long. I don't think you should—'

'I don't care what textbooks say, Leigh. And doctors have been wrong before.'

Yes, thought Leigh, they have. But her years of training made her feel sceptical about it.

'I still think—' she began, aware that Adam was waiting patiently in the hall.

'You know, I can almost feel a tingling in my hand already. I do believe I'm getting better!' Evelyn exclaimed.

'Well, don't start jogging around the block until I get back,' joked Leigh, and kissed her. 'Now I really must go. Your library book is on the television table, and the *Radio Times* is in the drawer.'

She hurried out to the hall, leaving her mother gazing at her hand, trying to flex the fingers.

'Everything all right?' asked Adam.

'Oh—yes—she was just fussing.' She must have sounded a little vague and distracted, because he gave her a speculative glance. But he said nothing, and she collected her suede jacket from the cloakroom and followed him out to his car.

Once they were on their way he glanced at her again and remarked, 'Your mother sounded excited. She wasn't upset, was she, because you were leaving her for the evening?'

73

'No, she wasn't upset. As a matter of fact—' She hesitated, and concentrated her gaze on his hands on the wheel.

'Yes?' They were driving along the main Oxford road now, moving in the direction of the city centre, some eight miles away. Mossgate was one of the larger suburbs, spreading from Kings Wood to the Worcester-shire border. They were travelling towards Kings Wood.

'She was a little excited. She'd remembered something from ten years ago.'

'I suppose she has no memory of her accident and operation,' said Adam, turning from the Oxford road into Links Lane.

'No. Quite a large chunk has been missing from her life. It makes her feel quite frustrated.'

'And now she's remembered something. I'm not surprised she's excited. What brought it on?'

'Seeing you.' Leigh felt a tightening in her chest. He smiled, but didn't seem to react.

'She's seen me before—bronchitis, if I recall. And some skin rash, I think it was. She usually sees Arthur Brent, but it isn't always possible.'

'I pointed out to her that she'd seen you fairly recently, but she was adamant that she saw you ten years ago. She says you were a doctor at the hospital when she had her operation.'

74

'The Queen Anne?'

'Yes.'

'Impossible. I've never worked at the Queen Anne. I trained in Nottingham, and did my house jobs up north. I've never worked at the Queen Anne.'

'She seemed so certain.'

He didn't answer, but stopped the car outside a cream stone building. A large wooden sign, which badly needed repainting, pronounced that it was the Mossgate community hall. Another notice, fixed to the wall, gave dates and times of various activities.

Once he'd locked the car, Adam turned to Leigh. 'It seems her memory is still rather faulty, Leigh. I shouldn't worry about it. Perhaps there was a doctor who looked very much like me—a sort of *déjà vu*—you know what I mean.'

Leigh felt oddly deflated. She nodded.

'How can I tell her her memory's still faulty, Adam? She was so thrilled that it was coming back.'

'I'm afraid there's little chance it will come back completely. Memory's a funny thing. She thinks she's seen me at the hospital, but it must have been someone else, believe me. You'll just have to be tactful.'

Leigh sighed as she followed him into the foyer of the hall. A large notice-board sported a variety of handwritten and typed posters and advertisements. A pram was for sale—folding type; also a three-piece suite—pink dralon. The Mossgate Male Voice Choir had cancelled its performance on October 2nd—long gone—because of illness. A whist drive was being held on September 24th. Underneath the last one, a small printed notice informed everyone that £57.39p had been raised for the Children's Hospice, from a jumble sale.

Leigh barely glanced at these snippets of information. She had just realised how much she had been hoping that her mother might improve. Evelyn had always talked about getting her memory back, remembering those missing months, and how happy she'd be. Tonight, Leigh had thought that prospect was in sight. And now, with a few short words, Adam had ended it all: 'I've never worked at the Queen Anne.' Her mother's memory was still at fault. She was not going to get better.

Adam pushed open the double swing doors, and Leigh followed him into the hall. Folding tables and tubular chairs lined the walls, except for the far end where a large stage was curtained in blue. On the left, an alcove with a closed hatch obviously led to the kitchen. Leigh had been in places like this before. The hall was probably large enough to seat two hundred people. At the thought of performing to two hundred people, she almost turned tail and fled.

But Adam had taken hold of her hand and was leading her towards a small group of people clustered round a table near the stage. They turned and looked at her curiously, and she gave a nervous smile.

'Behold the new Amanda,' Adam announced. 'Her name's Leigh.'

'Amanda?' shrieked a tall, black-haired girl. 'But I'm doing Amanda. Roger said I could.'

'But Sarah, you're doing Celia! You're almost word-perfect.'

'I know, but I've never liked the part. She's too drab. Amanda's much more interesting. More fun.' She giggled. 'More wicked.'

'More like you, I suppose,' murmured a fair girl with glasses.

Leigh took in at a glance the dark-haired girl's pretty, pouting mouth, her wide brown eyes, like a deer's, her pale creamy skin and well-cut hair. Sarah. And she had been Celia. Leigh felt a surge of relief. Sarah didn't want to be Celia any longer. She wanted to be Amanda. So where did that leave herself? Without a part? And she'd just got used to the idea!

Adam spread his hands and shrugged. 'Well, if you've made up your mind, Sarah, what can I do? I can't force you. And I can't possibly ask Leigh to take on the part of Celia; she's the main character—'

'Why not?' Leigh almost surprised herself. What was she thinking about? Less than three months to learn the lead, and she hadn't done any acting for about eight years. Yes,

Lower Sixth at Mercy Hill Girls' School. *Twelfth Night.* She'd played—yes—Viola. And Sebastian had been that tall girl in the Upper Sixth, the one who had run away with the music master.

'Do you think you could do it?' Adam was asking. 'I thought you'd be glad to get out of it.'

'I'm beginning to like the idea,' she admitted.

'You're an angel!' He kissed her on the cheek impulsively. Just then the doors swung open with a rush, and a stocky, balding individual in a cream polo-necked sweater and leather jacket came striding energetically across the floor. Sarah hurried towards him, laying a hand on his arm.

'We've got another Celia, Roger—Adam brought her. So now I'll have more time to help you direct. I shall really enjoy that.'

'I'm sure you will,' murmured Roger, turning from her and dumping his bag on the table. He produced a copy of the play for Leigh, and she sat down to read it. She didn't get very far before Roger called them to get started.

'Right, boys and girls, we'll do Act Two, Scene One tonight. Celia's just realised she's in danger of losing Rupert to Amanda, and decides to try desperate methods.'

Leigh tensed. What on earth did he mean, desperate methods? She hadn't read that far.

78

And she wondered what she'd let herself in for.

'Celia, you're on stage. You've witnessed a passionate scene between Rupert and Amanda. You're in a state. That's it—come on, look bothered. Good, that's good.'

Her script in one hand, Leigh read her lines aloud, trying to control her nervous trembling. This was like being at school again! As she read, her eyes were automatically registering what was coming. And she was beginning to regret her impulsive behaviour.

'So that's what he wants, is it? That's the sort of girl he really wants. Very well—that's the sort of girl he's going to get!'

She mimed pulling off her jacket and unfastening the buttons of a high-necked shirt. Inside she was cringing. This wasn't the sort of part she had in mind! A *femme fatale.* What would Adam think of her? Could this be why he'd suggested she play the part of Amanda? But no—she was supposed to be the scarlet woman, and Celia was— Sarah had called her drab.

Adam had stepped on to the stage now, and was looking horrified as she walked towards him.

'Why, Rupert, where did you get to? You've been simply ages!' She flung her arms around his neck and murmured, 'I've missed you.'

Oh, God, this was awful! thought Leigh. Why had he asked her? He must have known what it entailed.

He was hissing something at her, and she glanced quickly at her script. A kiss. They were supposed to kiss. Passionately. Holding her breath, she lifted her face to his, and his mouth met hers. She had imagined it would be difficult to simulate passion, but it wasn't as hard as all that. It wasn't anywhere near as terrible as she'd expected. His lips were soft and warm, his kiss was tender. She felt a stirring inside herself, a soft urge to melt into his arms, to respond . . .

'OK, Rupert,' came Roger's voice. But Adam continued to hold her closely, his lips prolonged their ardent contact. Leigh found herself wanting it to go on and on . . .

'You don't have to make a meal of her, Rupert! Don't forget, you're supposed to be shocked at her behaviour. She's been frigid up to now.'

Shaking, Leigh stepped back from Adam's embrace. He wasn't looking at Roger, but at her, and his eyes held an expression she hadn't seen before. She looked away and pretended to read her script. She could barely see the words, the way her hands were trembling.

'Sorry, Roger,' called Adam. 'Got a bit carried away. Shall we go through that bit again?' He glanced mischievously at Leigh, and she took a quick breath.

'We'd be here all night,' said Roger curtly. 'No, carry on from there. Act shocked. She's not the Celia you knew.'

Leigh swallowed and looked up at Adam. 'Didn't you miss me too, darling?'

'What sort of question is that?' he asked harshly, grabbing her arm. 'I suppose you sent that letter to Amanda?'

She stared at him. His eyes were blazing, his mouth taut. He didn't look like Adam Christie any more. Of course, he wasn't. He was Rupert Something-or-other, and he was an impressively good actor. So good an actor that she'd been fooled into thinking he meant that kiss. But he'd just been acting, as she had. Hadn't she?

'I don't know anything about a letter, Rupert,' she quoted sweetly, looking up at him. 'Only the love letters you sent me.' His hand was still on her arm, and his eyes were watching her intently, and they were so very blue . . .

*　　*　　*

'I fell,' moaned Evelyn. 'I tripped over the doormat by the front door.'

'What were you doing by the front door?'

Leigh glanced at Adam, who had followed her into the house and was standing in the hall. It was quite late, but she had felt obliged to ask him in for coffee, in return for bringing her home.

'I was looking for you,' said Evelyn. 'It was

late. I— Hello, Dr Christie. You didn't need to bring the doctor in, Leigh. I'm not hurt, just a bit shaken. Nothing's broken.'

'Well, now Dr Christie's here, Mother, do you want him to look at your leg?'

'It was my ankle—I expect I've bruised it. I hit it against the umbrella stand, great big heavy thing. I've been meaning to give it to Oxfam.'

Adam knelt by the sofa, and his long, experienced fingers gently massaged and kneaded the weak, thin ankle.

'I thought the feeling was coming back, I suppose,' said Evelyn. Leigh had intended to go and put the kettle on, but she felt mesmerised by the rhythmic movement of Adam's hands on her mother's ankle. Then he stood up.

'I can't feel any damage,' he announced. 'You'll probably have a nasty bruise. Try and rest it for a few days.'

'Will I be all right for a week tomorrow?' asked Evelyn. 'I'm thinking of going to Wales.'

'You should be all right by then.' He turned to Leigh. 'Are you going away too? Of course, you must be. For how long?'

But Leigh was equally mystified. 'I don't know anything about it! When was all this arranged, Mother? Who's taking you on holiday? Kate?'

'Dear me, Kate doesn't take holidays in October—Ricky's at school.'

'I thought perhaps it was half-term or something.'

'My friend Cora has been lent a cottage in the country, somewhere near Aberystwyth, I think. She asked me to go with her.'

'Why didn't you tell me, Mother?' sighed Leigh.

'She only rang today. I wasn't sure I'd go, but then I had that flash of memory, and I began to think a few days away might be just what I need. Did you tell Dr Christie, Leigh? About my memory?'

'Mother, I'm sure Dr Christie is anxious to get home.' Leigh flashed him a warning glance. But Evelyn was determined he should know.

'The Queen Anne Hospital it was, Dr Christie. I remember you quite clearly. But I don't suppose you remember me, do you? You see so many people.'

'You're right, I do see a lot of people. And it was a long time ago.'

'Ten years. But it's such a good sign, don't you think? I'm sure I'm going to get completely well. But I expect it will take time. I'll try not to rush things.'

'I'm sure it will take a long time,' Adam said tactfully, moving towards the door.

Well, thought Leigh, you got out of that very cleverly, Adam.

'I'll put the kettle on,' she offered.

'Please no, not for me. Your mother looks

83

very tired. She should be in bed. I'll see you tomorrow.'

She followed him to the front door. He spoke quietly. 'I don't think we should encourage this memory thing too much, Leigh. She's only going to be disappointed.' He opened the door. 'Thank you for coming tonight. And you were much better than I expected.'

He kissed her gently on the lips, and walked down the drive. Was I? thought Leigh. What exactly did he mean by that? He was very clever with words, she decided. He'd got out of an embarrassing situation very well, without even having to admit he didn't remember her mother at all. And, of course, he didn't, because he'd never seen her until he came to work in Mossgate.

She went back to the sitting-room, to help her mother to bed.

*   *   *

The antenatal clinic was almost over. It was midday, and just one patient remained in the waiting-room, a large lady with fair hair and pink cheeks. She wore a loose dress over jogging trousers, and bounced a baby on her knee. Leigh went across to her.

'Are you sure you're at the right clinic?' she asked. She didn't know the woman, yet if she was Dr Powell's patient she should be in her own files. The baby was young, about five or six months old, but far too fat. He gurgled happily as his mother jiggled him around.

'Isn't this Dr Powell's antenatal clinic?' said the woman.

'Yes. I'm sorry, I didn't realise you were—'

'Pregnant? Due next April. Oh, I know what you're thinking—it was an accident. But it wasn't. It was planned. I always intended to have two close together. I'm hoping for a girl, but I don't mind.'

'I'm glad,' said Leigh, adding tactfully, 'He's a very bonny baby. Does he like his food?'

'Like it? He lives for it. And all his bottles. I can't satisfy him.' The woman laughed. The baby chortled, burped, and was slightly sick over his mother's hand.

'Ugh!' said his mother cheerfully, wiping it away. Leigh stifled a comment that the baby was obviously being overfed. This was not the time nor the place, and both mother and baby seemed very happy. Better to keep the status quo. Time for advice when it was needed.

So she smiled at her, and chucked the baby under his chin. He gurgled again. He *was* a nice baby, she decided. Fat, but nice. Still, perhaps Dr Powell would say something. If she didn't, no doubt the woman would come to the well baby clinic. That would be the right time and the right place.

A student midwife was helping the doctor, so Leigh made her way back to the office, passing the doctors' waiting-room on the way. There were always people waiting here, whatever time one looked. And now Leigh noticed Mrs Fletcher, of yesterday's home visit. She was sitting alone, looking worried, an unopened magazine on her knee. But she smiled when Leigh went across to her.

'So you decided not to wait until next week,' said Leigh. Mrs Fletcher looked puzzled.

'You were going to see Dr Christie about your headaches next week,' Leigh reminded her. 'Is it very bad today?'

'I've really just come for some tablets.' She fiddled with a plastic Tesco carrier bag.

'For the headaches?'

'Fancy you remembering! Actually, it's not so bad today, but it's my stomach, a lot of colic. I thought I might be allergic to something.'

'I'm sure Dr Christie will sort it out for you, Mrs Fletcher. Oh—his light's come on.'

Mrs Fletcher stood up. 'I'm glad I'm the last patient. Perhaps he won't mind if I chat a bit.' She gave Leigh a nervous smile and went into the consulting-room. Leigh stood for a moment, thinking. Her first impression, that the woman had something on her mind, seemed to have been correct. She was definitely worried about something, and it was causing all these physical symptoms. Then she relaxed. It seemed Mrs Fletcher had decided to unburden herself to Dr Christie.

As she approached the office, Daphne Horton emerged from the clinic-room and took her arm.

'Come and see the set-up for the elderly activities session, Leigh. It's important you understand what it's all about. You may have a patient you want to attend.'

Leigh followed her into the large room, which was also used for the two handicapped groups, and the well baby clinic. The chairs had been arranged so that part of the room was clear.

'Some do the exercises sitting down,' Daphne explained. 'The others stand. We have music, and relaxation. And the physiotherapist is here, for those who need her. Strange how the men seem to have lots of aches and pains.' They laughed. 'You'll want to get off home for lunch,' said Daphne. 'How's your mother?'

'She's fine—oh, she tripped and bruised her ankle yesterday. But Adam—Dr Christie—looked at it. Nothing damaged, he said.'

'You fetched him out to see her?'

Leigh flushed. 'Well, not really. I was with him at the time. He asked me to join the Mossgate Players.'

Daphne laughed. 'He's roped you in for that pretty smartish. He once asked me. And Pauline. He asks everyone—I should have warned you. Still, I'm sure you came to no harm.'

I'm not so sure, thought Leigh. 'I quite

87

enjoyed it,' she admitted. 'Adam's a very good actor—quite professional.' Oh, yes, quite professional.

'I can believe that. He's got a certain charisma. Oh, talk of the devil—'

Adam Christie was walking towards them. 'I have to talk to you, Leigh,' he said, in a serious tone. Leigh felt a flicker of apprehension.

'Mrs Fletcher?' she asked. He frowned, and glanced at Daphne.

'Yes—Mrs Fletcher. Will you come along to my room?'

Not sure whether she should feel excited or worried, Leigh followed him inside, and he closed the door behind them.

'Hey, don't look so worried! I don't bite!' he laughed.

'I was—just thinking about Mrs Fletcher,' she fibbed. 'She seemed very worried about something. What did she tell you?'

'Oh—some nervous indigestion. I gave her some antacid, but I couldn't get her to tell me what was really wrong.'

Leigh sighed with relief. 'So you agree there's something worrying her. But she wouldn't tell you? I wonder if she'll tell me?'

'Why don't you try?' he asked.

'I will. Well, if that's all you want to say, I'd better go. I can't think why you had to bring me here just to tell me that.'

Adam sat at his desk, pushing the chair back and stretching out his legs.

'Sit down, Leigh. I didn't bring you here to talk about Mrs Fletcher. I said that to get rid of Daphne. I want you and your mother to come down to Stow on Sunday.'

Leigh sank into the other chair. 'To Stow? Why?'

'I want to give you both a day out. Your mother needs a change of air. She's very pale.'

'She may go to Wales next week.'

'Yes, I know. But I'd like her to meet my mother. My mother has mobility problems, but she's quite a few years older than yours.'

'Arthritis?' she queried.

He nodded. 'Osteoarthritis, mainly in her hips. Some days are better than others.'

'I'm trying to persuade Mother to come to the Tuesday club here,' Leigh told him. 'She didn't actually refuse, so I suppose there's a chance she may agree. She's always found difficulty in coming to terms with her limited mobility. I suppose that's why she was so excited yesterday when she thought her memory was coming back.'

'That's quite understandable,' he agreed.

'But, of course, it isn't coming back, as you pointed out to me. You never were at the Queen Anne.'

He looked quizzically at her. 'Don't you believe me?'

'I want to believe you. But Mother was so adamant she'd seen you before.'

'Obviously confusing me with those times I

89

went to visit her. Leigh, you must trust me. I've never worked at the Queen Anne, I promise.'

His gaze held hers, unblinking, his eyes the colour of a summer sky. She was the first to look away, her hazel eyes troubled.

'We shouldn't allow her to delude herself,' she said. 'I noticed when she told you she'd seen you before you didn't contradict her. But you didn't admit she had either.'

'You're very astute, Leigh.' He stood up, and she was aware of his masculinity, his air of authority. 'I'll pick you both up at eleven o'clock on Sunday,' he said. 'Wear some strong shoes, as I intend to show you the magnificent views from Deepwater.'

'Is that far?' she asked.

'Deepwater is our house. It was built just after the war, not far from the Stow Wells, where the town used to get its water supply. The well is still there.'

'And my mother?'

'She can talk to my mother. And Father can show her the garden.'

The conversation seemed to be at an end. Leigh stood up.

'I'm sure we shall both enjoy—' she began, but her words were abruptly cut short by Adam's mouth on hers. His hands held her shoulders firmly, and she held her breath for a moment. But the kiss was brief, and when he stepped back he looked rather sheepish.

'I'm sorry, Leigh, I took advantage of you.

What a good thing you're not my patient!'

Leigh trembled slightly as she said, 'Why, do you do this to all your patients? Is it a new sort of therapy?'

'Don't joke about it. I've apologised. It's just that—well, for a moment you looked rather as Celia did last night, when you were on the stage, all flushed and golden-eyed, and I got carried away. Please forget it happened.'

Leigh seemed to feel a great hollow inside. It wasn't her he felt the urge to kiss, just a character in a play. Not a real person at all. And, of course, he was allowed to kiss Celia whenever he wanted to. She felt a surge of indignation rising up.

'And is it Celia you want to take to Stow on Sunday? Is it Celia you want your mother to meet? I'm not Celia, Adam, I'm Leigh, and I'm real, and I don't like to be mistaken for a fantasy person. If you want to kiss me, go ahead, but make sure you know *who* you're kissing—Leigh Rochester!'

She felt breathless, and her heart was racing. She was sure she'd said too much, sure he would withdraw his invitation. Why was she so determined to spoil things?

Adam didn't even look angry. He gently lifted her chin and looked deep into her eyes. She couldn't breathe.

'Is that what you thought, Leigh? That I was confusing fact with fantasy? I'm only too aware that you're real—too real for comfort, when

91

you look at me with those tawny eyes. Why do you think I didn't want you to take the part of Celia? Because I knew it involved so many romantic scenes, and I didn't want to give myself away too soon. But I did, didn't I?'

'You mean—that kiss last night—you meant it?' Her mouth felt dry, and there was a singing in her ears.

'Of course I meant it. As I mean this one.' He drew her into his arms and his lips closed over hers. This time Leigh gave herself up to her instincts; she felt her body melt into his, her lips merge into his kiss. She began to feel she was drowning, as feelings she didn't even know she possessed swept over her, submerging her conscious mind, transforming her body into one mass of throbbing sensation.

She was shaking as he finally released her. He was breathing fast, and his blue eyes glittered.

'Was that Leigh I just kissed? Or Celia?' he said huskily. His eyes looked like sapphires.

'Leigh,' she whispered, nestling into his arms.

'So you weren't pretending, either, last night.'

'No. I thought you were just a very good actor.'

'Not that good, I'm afraid. Ask Sarah.'

Leigh had never thought of herself as a jealous person. But the realisation that Sarah too had been kissed by those lips—and many more times too—brought back the feeling of envy she'd had last night. But surely Sarah wasn't a rival? She seemed to be in love with Roger.

The intercom buzzed just then. Adam pressed a button, and the voice of a receptionist came over clearly.

'I didn't know you were still in the building, Dr Christie. I have a call for you—Dr Pritchard at the Queen Anne.'

'Put him through,' said Adam warmly, settling in his chair. He picked up the external phone. 'Dr Pritchard, Christie here. What can I do for you?'

Leigh stood waiting, uncertain as to whether she should leave or stay. It didn't seem to be a personal call, but she felt she was eavesdropping. She watched Adam's expression as he talked, his laughing blue eyes as he listened to some amusing anecdote, his mobile, sensual mouth, those soft lips that had just kissed her so passionately. She felt hot colour rising. She shouldn't stay while he talked. She rested her hand on the door-handle. He glanced towards her and she paused. He made a gesture with his free hand. Was he asking her to stay? His fingers were long, his hands tanned. On the third finger of his right hand he wore a gold signet-ring with a diamond in the middle. The third finger.

Leigh recalled Pauline's words yesterday . . . a confirmed bachelor . . . some sad love-affair in his youth.

Did that mean he had sworn off women for good? Was she hoping for too much? Quietly she opened the door and slipped out.

CHAPTER SIX

Adam didn't appear to notice Leigh's exit. He was still busily discussing the advantages of the latest anti-depressants.

Leigh sat at her desk and stared at the papers in front of her. Was she making premature assumptions of his feelings towards her?

You're jumping the gun, girl, she admonished herself. Just because he enjoyed kissing you. What's in a kiss, anyway? Did he say he loved you? Of course he didn't. Love doesn't enter into it. How can it? We first met ten days ago. He was impressed with your resuscitation technique. You took a fancy to his blue eyes and his sensual mouth. She shivered. Yes, he knew how to use that sensual mouth, didn't he?

She gave herself a mental shake. He just finds you attractive, that's all. Don't let yourself fall for his kisses and his romantic talk. He's a good actor, that's all. A very good actor.

She glanced at her watch. Twelve thirty-five.

Daphne had gone to lunch; her timetable never varied. Leigh pushed her papers together and stood up. She flicked through her files. Who was she due to visit this afternoon? Should she stop off at Sainsbury's and get her mother some ham for her lunch? Or some fish?

The door opened quietly. She looked up. Adam came towards her, and she couldn't stop the little flutter that ran through her.

'I wondered where you'd gone,' he said quietly. He looked straight into her eyes.

'I dislike overhearing private conversations.'

'It was purely professional,' he said casually. 'Sunday at eleven, then?'

She nodded. 'Sunday at eleven.' He moved as if to kiss her, but she deliberately bent her head and picked out a card. For a moment he didn't move, then he crossed to the door. Leigh looked up. 'I'm looking forward to it.'

He seemed about to say something, but someone passed the door and spoke to him. He turned and left.

I shall look on it as a professional visit to help my mother, thought Leigh. With no expectations.

*   *   *

Sunday was one of those rare golden October days, with the sun shining on the red and yellow leaves that had begun to form a carpet on the lawns and pavements.

'What shall I wear?' asked Evelyn for the third time.

'I told you—that grey silk dress with the little crimson leaves on it. It's always suited you.'

'But it's old! I wish you'd given me more notice, Leigh. I'd have bought a new one.'

Leigh laughed. 'You don't need a new one, Mother. You're not going to a Royal garden party!'

'And what shall you wear?' Evelyn turned her attention to Leigh, who was fresh from the shower, her skin flushed, her nut-brown hair clinging to her neck.

'Adam suggested showing me the sights, so I'd better wear something sensible. I thought my green skirt and my Fair Isle sweater. And my flat shoes.'

She began to gather her hair into its usual style at the back of her neck. No point in trying to impress him.

'Aren't you leaving your hair loose?' her mother asked.

'I think there's a wind getting up, and I get irritated when my hair flies into my face. Besides, this visit isn't for my benefit, it's for you.'

Evelyn laughed. 'Is that what he told you? Well, I've heard other excuses, but it's the first time I've heard the mother given as a reason for courting.'

Leigh laughed at the old-fashioned word. 'Courting? Adam isn't courting me. We're just colleagues. He thought you looked pale and needed a change of air, and I agree with him. It's nothing more. I'm just coming along for the ride.'

Evelyn gave her a strange look but said nothing. She rummaged around on the dressing-table. 'Where's my garnet brooch?' she muttered.

Leigh found it, and pinned it at the neckline of her mother's silk dress. She stood back and looked at her. 'You look lovely. Perhaps it's really you he likes.'

'Don't be silly. By the way, you didn't tell me how the play rehearsal went. Did you get the part of Amanda?'

'No, I was coerced into taking the lead. I wish I hadn't agreed.' Leigh glanced at her mother. 'I see you're walking better.'

'Changing the subject again. I shall never walk better while this wretched leg is so weak.'

'It could be worse. You ought to come to the Tuesday club. You'd be positively agile compared with some of them. We have amputees, strokes, fractured spines—now paraplegics. And they aren't all elderly, you know. Some are a lot younger than you. And they really seem to enjoy life. Of course, Graham's very good. He gets them going.'

'Is he disabled?' asked Evelyn.

'He doesn't appear to be. I don't know

much about him. But I've met him, and what I've seen I've liked. He seemed genuine, sincere, kind-hearted.' Leigh looked away. 'A lot like Daddy.'

Evelyn gave a sigh. 'It's too much to hope there'd be another like him,' she said softly. Leigh squeezed her shoulder.

'No one expects you to forget Daddy, but it is eight years, and you've got a lot of your life left. Please think about coming on Tuesday.'

Evelyn was silent for a moment. She sighed again. 'I'll think about it,' she promised.

*   *   *

Evelyn settled herself comfortably into the back of Adam's BMW. Leigh, in the passenger seat, flashed her a smile before fastening her seatbelt. Adam started the car, and inserted a cassette into the player. Soft music soon filled the car. They moved away, along Banbury Road.

Leigh felt awkward. She knew she ought to make conversation, but she couldn't think what to say. Adam had barely spoken to her since he'd arrived, but had fussed around her mother. Leigh guessed he was regretting that kiss in his surgery. Oh, well, she'd just have to make the best of it.

'Do we go through Evesham?' she asked brightly. He glanced at her.

'Not exactly through it. I use the bypass to

Broadway.'

'I stayed in Broadway once,' said Evelyn chattily. 'When I was young. I expect it's changed a lot since then.'

'Broadway's a place that never changes,' said Adam. 'And certainly not in a few years.'

'Flatterer!' laughed Evelyn. 'I'm talking about the fifties.'

'We-ell, probably not as many tourist shops then. Antique shops and souvenir shops. But I doubt if the old Cotswold stone buildings have changed. It's very much like Stow.'

They chatted easily for a while, Evelyn talking about her teenage years, when she'd done a little nursing but gave it up on a sudden impulse after an altercation with one of the sisters.

'A right tartar she was,' she said vehemently. 'She made all the girls' lives a misery. You couldn't do anything right. Well, I decided I wasn't going to stand for it, so I walked out, and she had to do the bedpans herself!' she chortled.

'It sounds as if you had plenty of spirit in those days,' said Adam.

'Yes, I did have spirit, and I wasn't going to let Sister Savident drive it out of me. I went to work in an office. Mind you, that wasn't much better. But at least I met Tom.'

'Savident?' queried Adam. 'Esme Savident? Tall, olive-skinned, crooked teeth?'

'That's the one!' cried Evelyn. 'Do you

99

know her? If all we nurses had had our wish she'd have dropped dead within the year. She's not still around?'

'I met her at Nottingham University Hospital. She was a senior nursing officer. Probably retired by now.'

'I was at Nottingham General,' said Evelyn. 'She must have moved. Perhaps they turfed her out. She caused a lot of girls to leave.'

'I can imagine that,' said Adam.

They were approaching Evesham. Leigh had been content to snuggle into her seat and listen sleepily to her mother's talking. As they turned on to the Evesham bypass, Evelyn said, 'Fancy you working at Nottingham.'

'I trained there,' said Adam shortly. 'And I did my house jobs in Sheffield and Manchester.'

'But you didn't like the north,' said Evelyn.

'Quite the contrary. I really enjoyed the years I worked in the north.'

'So what else did you do there?' queried Leigh. 'After your resident posts.'

'I was a locum for a while in a practice in Salford. Just a small practice with three doctors.'

The conversation seemed to pall then, as they followed the main road to Broadway. Once they arrived in the small town, Evelyn became excited, pointing out various shops and buildings.

'Oh, yes, I remember that shop. And that

house. I think an old lady lived there alone—Miss Foxglove, or something.'

'Foxglove!' laughed Adam and Leigh.

'Well, something like that.'

Leigh turned to glance at her mother, who was suddenly sounding younger. And happier. She looked happier too, and her eyes seemed to have a sparkle she hadn't seen for a long time.

They drove along the main street of Broadway, on into the countryside beyond. The views were magnificent, and Leigh was grateful for the opportunity to look at them. When she was driving, her gaze had always been directed at the road ahead, with no chance to admire the tranquil green and yellow fields, the patchwork quilt of hedges and meadows, dotted with the white of sheep, the black and white of Friesian cattle.

Evelyn started to talk again, this time about the war, when she was a child. But she sounded lethargic, and eventually even that subject seemed to lose its interest for her. When Leigh glanced back at her, her mother's eyes were closed.

'You're very quiet,' said Adam softly, and glanced quickly at her.

'It's that sort of day,' she said, not really knowing what she meant.

But Adam nodded. 'I suppose it is.'

'Mother seems to be enjoying herself.' She mustn't forget this day was for her benefit.

'She's gone to sleep, I should imagine.'

'I think she was quite excited. She sounded the way she used to before she had her accident and operation.'

As if in reply, on the back seat Evelyn gave a soft little snore.

'I'd like to hear about it,' said Adam quietly.

'It was ten years ago. We didn't even know Mother was feeling ill. She may have mentioned the occasional headache, and I don't suppose we took much notice. But they must have been worse than she let on, because the doctor at the hospital wrote it in—' Leigh paused, afraid to admit she'd read her mother's notes.

'Yes?' prompted Adam.

'Well, it was suggested she may have been feeling dizzy when she stepped off the bus, and straight under the wheels of a lorry. She had concussion, and then compression, so they rushed her into Theatre. And when they operated they found a large tumour in her brain. They managed to remove it, but it left her with paralysis on her left side. They felt she may never walk again.'

There was a short silence, as Adam overtook a tractor.

'So it was a blessing in disguise,' he suggested.

'A blessing? I don't understand. They should have found it earlier.'

'How could they? If she kept it to herself,

and it sounds as though she did, how could they know? You said yourself you didn't even know she was feeling ill. You know, it sounds to me as though you're trying to put the blame on the doctors.' He sounded amazed at her temerity.

It was an effort to keep her voice low. 'I just feel it could have been found earlier, that's all. Before she had her accident . . .'

'And suppose she told no one? She didn't tell her family.'

'No. But I happen to know she did see someone. Not her own GP, but his locum. And he didn't even think to refer her to a specialist. Put it down to her age. Naturally I blame that doctor—oh, not for the whole thing, that would be silly, but for the delay in getting her to hospital. She could have died in the accident! Wouldn't you blame him, in my position?'

Adam kept his eyes on the road and didn't answer. Then he said slowly, 'A locum? Are you sure about that?'

'Positive.'

He didn't answer, and manoeuvred a sharp bend in the road.

'I take it she remembers little of that period,' he said, his eyes on the road ahead. They passed a signpost for Stow-on-the-Wold, then a hamlet of yellow stone houses.

'She remembers nothing—I told you that. She thought she remembered you, but of course she didn't.'

'No. Well, we're almost there.' They had reached the junction of the main road with the Fosse Way. Ahead was the High Street, leading to the Square. It was beginning to look quite familiar to Leigh. She recalled her first visit, and the way Adam had walked briskly away after Mr Keith had been taken to hospital. So she wasn't surprised when he now steered the car in the same direction, around Parsons Corner. To the right was the town, and lots of new housing. Evelyn stirred on the back seat.

'Are we there? I must have dropped off.'

'Almost, Mother,' Leigh told her.

The lane was narrow, with views of Stow and the surrounding areas on the right, and steep banks on the left. They passed what appeared to be a giant horse trough, with water cascading into it.

'Stow Wells,' said Adam. 'And here we are.'

A wide curving drive ended at a large house of Cotswold Stone, with an imposing Doric-style doorway, and extensive windows on either side. Adam stopped the car.

'This is Deepwater House.'

Leigh helped her mother from the car and up the two steps to the house. The sun shone golden on the mellow stone of the walls. The trees edging the drive were bronze and amber, the lawns sage and ochre.

'An autumn house,' Leigh murmured to

herself.

'I've always felt the same,' said Adam at her shoulder. 'Come on inside.'

Moving slowly to accommodate Evelyn's halting walk, they followed him into a large sunny morning-room.

'Mother, this is Leigh, and her mother Mrs Rochester. My mother.'

Grace Christie was still quite tall and imposing, despite the fact that she leaned heavily on a stick. Her grey hair was brushed back from her face, her blue eyes—just like Adam's, Leigh thought—alert behind gold-rimmed spectacles. She wore a dark blue Paisley dress with a light blue shawl pinned with a silver brooch.

She held out her hand to Evelyn, who took it hesitantly. 'I expected you to be in a wheelchair,' Grace said. 'You've been very brave to negotiate our gravel drive.'

'I'm not paralysed,' said Evelyn, a little indignantly. 'Just a slight weakness I have in my leg.'

'Then we're quits.' Grace looked hard at Leigh. 'And you're Leigh.' She held out her hand, and Leigh took it. It was strong and warm, no weakness there.

'How are you, Mrs Christie?' smiled Leigh.

'Not one of my better days, but I daren't complain. Tomorrow might be worse.' She gave a dry laugh. 'Won't you sit down? I'll see if Mrs Dunn is ready.'

105

'I'll do that, Mother,' said Adam, moving away, and left Leigh and her mother to follow Mrs Christie into the sitting-room. It was high-ceilinged and sunny.

'Come and tell me about yourselves,' invited Grace.

Leigh tried to make sure her mother sat next to Mrs Christie, but Grace caught her eye and patted the chair nearest herself.

'You're a health visitor, Adam tells me.'

Leigh didn't want the conversation to revolve around herself—the visit was for her mother's benefit. But she couldn't help feeling as though they had been summoned to the presence of royalty. It reminded Leigh of those days long ago, when she'd been sent to Matron. This wasn't Matron, of course, but it felt the same.

She smiled and said, 'That's right. I've been working in Bath. I came back to Mossgate to help my mother, now my sister's gone to Oxford.'

'University?'

'Oh, no, she's married. They've gone to live in Oxford because of John's promotion. Kate has always looked after Mother.' Leigh glanced at Evelyn, who nodded and smiled.

Grace leaned forward. 'Was it a stroke?'

'Didn't Adam tell you?' said Evelyn. 'I had a very risky brain operation a few years ago, and it left me paralysed.'

'But you can still walk? You walked into this

house.'

'It's not nearly as bad as it was,' Evelyn admitted. 'But it took a long time to reach the state of improvement I've got today.'

'Like me, I expect you have your good days and your bad days,' smiled Grace Christie.

'But it doesn't stop you doing things,' said Adam from the doorway.

'Why should it? My mind hasn't gone yet. Now, if lunch is ready we'll go through and do justice to it. Did she finally decide to do the prawn salad, Adam?'

'Yes, Mother,' replied Adam, as they entered the dining-room across the wide hall. 'And egg mayonnaise, celery soup, granary bread—'

'That sounds fine. Perhaps you'd care to sit by me, Mrs Rochester?'

Leigh wondered if the seating arrangements had been made beforehand by Adam, because before she had time to take her seat next to her mother Mr Christie suddenly appeared, and she found herself sitting between the two men.

James Christie, a retired solicitor, a broad, ruddy-faced man with a thatch of fair hair fading into white, flirted outrageously with Leigh all through the meal, and Leigh, already feeling a little bothered, was forced to turn to Adam for moral support. She was relieved to see that Evelyn and Grace were getting on quite well together, and more than once she heard her father's name mentioned. It was a good thing, she thought, to get her mother to talk about him. And Grace Christie, with her solid commonsense attitude, would surely change her mother's negative way of thinking.

Adam frequently caught Leigh's eye, and once he winked at her, which sent a funny sort of thrill through her. But she was still determined to remain immune to his expressive blue eyes and the humorous quirk of his sensuous mouth.

Just as she was beginning to relax in their company, there was a lull in the conversation, and Grace looked across at Adam.

'Did you know Fenella's back from Africa, Adam?' she asked him.

'Fenella? No, I didn't.'

'I thought she may have got in touch with you.'

'I think that's highly unlikely.'

Grace glanced at Leigh before turning back to Adam with a smile. 'Do you think she's come back for good?' she asked.

Adam gave an exasperated sigh. 'I haven't the faintest idea. And I don't intend to give it another thought.'

'Good,' said James Christie briskly.

Grace shrugged her shoulders. 'Have you decided yet whether you're going to take another partner into the practice, Adam?'

'Oh, we definitely shall. In fact, we're seeing someone next week.'

The conversation began to settle into a comfortable rut, about work, and neighbours and friends, and finally turned to the family, and Adam mentioned his two younger brothers, both married. Mr Christie gave him a few bald hints that it was about time he settled down, but Adam just winked at Leigh and wouldn't be drawn.

'Not found the right girl, eh?' James Christie persisted.

'James!' his wife admonished him, glancing quickly at Leigh. 'That's not very tactful.'

James Christie turned to Leigh, grinning broadly. 'Sorry, my dear!'

Adam laid down his knife. 'I refuse to answer that question, Father, in case it incriminates me.' He refused to look at Leigh.

So that's that, thought Leigh, a cold lump of ice settling inside her. Despite what he had said in his consulting-room, he obviously had no intention of committing himself yet. And she wished Pauline had told her about his past before she'd let that kiss go to her head.

Lunch over, Grace took Evelyn into the garden to look at the new summer-house. James made some excuse and went off to his study.

'He's writing his memoirs,' Adam explained. 'I've told him it's a waste of time. Who wants to read the boring cases of a country solicitor?' He laughed. 'Actually, they're quite funny. But let's not talk about him. Let's go and look at

Stow Wells, and the views.' He took Leigh's hand, and they went to slip on their jackets.

Now Leigh had made up her mind she was not going to take Adam seriously, she began to enjoy his company. And as long as she didn't forget, and look too long into his eyes, she'd be all right.

They talked trivia as they walked along, and Adam pointed out various places of interest. The well—and Leigh thought again how much like a huge water trough it was—was set into the steep side of the lane. She climbed up to get a better look, and suddenly her foot slipped on the damp grass, twisted as she tried vainly to regain her balance, and she skidded awkwardly to the bottom. It had happened so quickly that Adam, standing above her, had been unable to grab her in time. He was swift to help her to her feet. As she put her weight on the twisted ankle, she let out a yelp of pain.

'You're hurt! Here, let me see. What have you done?' The concern in his voice seemed genuine.

'It's my ankle—I think I've sprained it.'

'That's my fault for bringing you along here. I might have guessed it would be slippery. Sit there. Let me see.'

'It's not your fault,' she protested, as he pulled off her shoe and began to examine her ankle. She giggled. 'Perhaps it runs in the family.'

'Let's hope you recover as quickly as your

mother did.' His touch was cool and gentle, his long fingers probing the joint expertly. And she wondered if her mother had felt as she did now, her skin tingling at his touch, her heart racing.

'Try to stand,' he advised her. 'I'm sure it isn't sprained.'

The ache was lessening already. He helped her to her feet, and held her as she attempted to put her weight on it.

'It's not too painful,' she gasped, suddenly finding it difficult to breathe. If only he wouldn't hold her so closely. She could feel the rough wool of his jacket, his breath on her face. He smelled nice . . .

'Feeling better?' he asked softly. She nodded, unable to speak. It's all my fault you're hurt,' he murmured, turning her to face him. And she couldn't help but look into those sky-blue eyes, and see the distress in them. She had heard the solicitude in his voice, but had told herself it was merely the concern any doctor had for a patient. His eyes told a different story. She looked deeply into them, and felt all her resolutions fade.

She swallowed. 'Please don't blame yourself—' she began, but Adam didn't seem to be listening. His blue eyes had darkened as he gently caressed her neck, loosening the ribbon that held back her hair. Leigh couldn't breathe. This wasn't why she'd come. This wasn't meant to happen!

'Adam—don't do this—don't say anything—'

'Why not? Are you afraid? Are you afraid I might say I love you?'

'Yes—no—' She felt so confused. Yet deep down she longed for him to hold her tight, to kiss her again and again . . .

'Don't be afraid,' he whispered. 'I'm not going to say it—it's too soon. But there's a distinct possibility I could fall in love with you, Leigh. A distinct possibility.'

CHAPTER SEVEN

Leigh's heart was pounding. He could easily fall in love with her! And it would be very easy to fall in love with him. If she hadn't done it already. Suddenly she felt the urge to tell him how she felt. Just as suddenly something stopped her. She felt that if she spoke words of love fate would step in and change everything. Spoil everything. And she didn't want to spoil this moment with mere words.

She moved slowly into Adam's embrace, and his lips gently touched her face, her neck, and then, as if waiting made fulfilment more sweet, his mouth gently touched hers. It was like a butterfly wing at first, a wisp of sensation brushing them innocently, yet the feeling seemed to stir in her longings she had never felt before, emotions that urged to be fulfilled.

112

The pressure of his lips became firmer, stronger, more passionate, and her own response was instinctive. All she was aware of was a burning, a searing, a volcano.

She was trembling when he finally released her, and she was amazed to see that the town below her still looked the same, the sun still glinted between the trees, the breeze still played with her hair. His arms were still warm around her, she could smell his musky after-shave, feel his jacket against her neck.

Was this love? She only knew she'd never experienced it before. Oh, she'd played at loving in the past, had been hurt when things had gone wrong. But never this—this aching to be touched, to be held, to be made love to. Her cheeks suddenly flamed at the thought. Whatever was she thinking? Adam hadn't said he loved her; he'd made a point of that. He'd said he *could* fall in love with her. It wasn't the same thing at all. Yet she knew in that instant that it was too late for her to back away, too late to accept him just as a friend. If he found he couldn't love her after all—

She swallowed, and smiled brightly at him. Better not to give her true feelings away just yet. Better to be sure.

She was sure.

Adam kissed her nose. 'I'll show you the town,' he said. 'Do you think you can walk now?'

Leigh gently tested her ankle. It seemed

113

stronger. And she recalled a phrase from the Bible—'. . . whither thou goest, I will go.' And she knew if Adam asked she would follow him anywhere.

'My ankle feels fine,' she said.

*   *   *

There wasn't enough time to see the whole town, but they did manage to look at the carvings on the headstone of the Cross in the Square, the yew trees round the door of the north porch of St Edward's Church, and a brief look at Fountain Court.

'I'll show you more next time you come,' Adam promised, as they walked slowly back to Deepwater House. Next time? thought Leigh. He intended to bring her again?

Her ankle was aching slightly again by the time they entered the house. It was quite late in the afternoon, and Mrs Dunn had laid out tea in the conservatory. Evelyn and Grace talked and laughed together, and Leigh was sure her mother seemed brighter and more cheerful.

Once tea was over, James took Evelyn to see his vinery, on the more sheltered south side of the house, and Adam made some excuse to go upstairs. Leigh was left with Grace Christie in the sitting-room, and she felt uncomfortable. Grace gave her a shrewd glance.

114

'Did you enjoy your walk?' she asked.

'Yes, thank you. Adam showed me the town—some of it.'

'Adam's very fond of Stow. We all are. This will be Adam's house one day, if he wants it.'

'How could he refuse it?' smiled Leigh.

'His career may take him out of the country. He's ambitious, you know. I don't imagine he'll be content to stay a Midlands general practitioner.'

'I thought he was quite happy in his work,' said Leigh. 'He seems to be quite dedicated.'

'He's dedicated to medicine. Hasn't he ever talked to you about this?'

How could he? thought Leigh apprehensively. I hardly know him. I love him, but I hardly know him.

'We haven't talked much about careers,' she said carefully.

'Of course not—I was forgetting. You haven't been long in Mossgate, have you?' said Grace.

'Not this time. But it is my home town. It's just that I've been away, in Bath.'

'So you said. A pleasant city, Bath. I know it quite well.'

'Yes. I enjoyed working there,' said Leigh.

'But you're going back, surely. Isn't this job only temporary?'

'Yes—I came to cover maternity leave. Six months.'

'Is that so? I don't want to sound prying,

Leigh, but your mother did mention someone—a librarian, I think she said.'

'Colin?' Leigh couldn't understand why Grace Christie was so interested in her private life. It wasn't as though she was here to be examined by prospective parents-in-law. Unless—unless that was how Grace saw it. Perhaps she thought Adam had brought them both down for Leigh's benefit, not her mother's. She opened her mouth to explain how it really was, but Grace was leaning forward in her chair, her gaze intent on Leigh's face.

'That's right,' she said quietly. 'Colin. Tell me about him.'

'He—he's just a friend, nothing more. And that's the truth.'

Grace sat back and a sigh escaped her. 'You're probably wondering why I'm asking you all these questions—aren't you?'

'Well—yes—' Leigh began.

'I don't know how you feel about my son, but I do get the distinct impression you're quite fond of him.'

Leigh was powerless to stop the wave of colour that flooded her cheeks. Was it so obvious?

'I like him—a lot,' she said cautiously. 'We seem to work well together. But Mrs Christie, really, that isn't the reason we've come down here. It was meant as an outing for my mother.'

'Oh, I see. I wasn't aware of that. Adam merely said he was bringing some friends down to see me. And of course, when I saw you, and the way he—' Grace stopped, and fiddled with the brooch on her shawl. Leigh stayed silent, sensing there was more to come. Grace Christie looked up and smiled.

'To tell you the truth, I was trying to warn you,' she confessed.

'Warn me? About what?'

'I don't want either of you to get hurt.'

'I don't understand.'

'No,' sighed Grace, 'I don't suppose you do. Haven't you stopped to wonder why a charming, attractive young man like Adam— and I'm not flattering him—is still unmarried at thirty-five?'

Leigh honestly hadn't thought much about it, until Pauline had mentioned the sad love-affair in his youth. At the outset she had imagined him to be a family man, hadn't she? He had seemed to be the marrying sort.

'Only vaguely,' she admitted.

'It isn't that he hasn't had the opportunities,' Grace told her, and her voice took on a confidential tone. 'He's had a number of female friends.'

Leigh had an awful thought that Mrs Christie was going to tell her things that Adam wouldn't want her to know. She spoke nervously. 'Mrs Christie, I don't know what you're about to tell me, but I have a feeling I really should hear it from Adam, if it's important.'

Grace Christie gave a short laugh. 'Adam will never tell you. He's too proud. And it isn't a secret—it's something you should know.'

'Is it—something that happened when he was much younger?'

'There you are, you see? You have been told.'

'No—not really. It was just a hint, that's all. And I can't imagine why everyone thinks I should know.'

'Can't you?' said Grace Christie softly. 'I wonder. You see, lots of women have been in love with Adam. I could see it on their faces.'

Leigh stared at the carpet, hoping her own face wasn't giving too much away to this discerning woman.

'They got hurt,' Grace said simply. 'Adam wasn't in love with them. He's been in love only once, and that was many years ago, when he was newly qualified. Fenella was a medical student. They seemed to be ideally suited. He brought her here many times, and I grew very fond of her.' Her voice seemed to harden. 'Adam asked her to marry him as soon as she qualified. She agreed. Plans were being made. Then, without warning, she went to Africa to work, and never came back. Until now.'

Leigh recalled the conversation at lunch, the guarded reaction from Adam.

'She jilted him?'

'She jilted him. Wrote to him from Africa saying she wasn't ready for marriage, she wanted to do something useful with her life. That was the only letter she wrote.'

'Poor Adam!'

'Quite,' said Grace drily. 'Do you understand why I'm telling you this?'

'You think he may still be in love with her?'

Grace was vehement. 'Oh, no, it's not that at all. But he was badly hurt, and it scarred him. He's been happier lately, and I did wonder—' She looked hard at Leigh. 'I don't want another girl to let him down, to hurt him like that again. He's still vulnerable. And if he's not yet ready to commit himself again, then I wanted to warn you. I don't want you to get hurt.'

A warm, grateful feeling flowed through Leigh. She leaned forward and touched Grace Christie's twisted hand.

'That's very kind of you. I promise you, I shall do all I can not to hurt him. That is—if he does ever fall in love with me.'

'But surely—' Grace began urgently, leaning forward. She started as the door behind them opened and Adam entered. He came and stood by Leigh, and she was acutely aware of his closeness.

'Chinwagging over?' he asked lightly, and his blue eyes met Leigh's. 'I suppose you've heard all about my misspent youth. I shall never live it down.'

119

Leigh sensed the pain behind the superficial manner.

'Your name did crop up in the conversation,' she admitted, trying to match his banter. He came and sat next to her, changing the subject adroitly. Leigh was only conscious of his body so close to hers, the warmth of his thigh against her. She was relieved that Grace Christie seemed to like her. But it was far too soon to tell her how she really felt. She hadn't even told Adam. She turned to look at him.

He was leaning forward to make a point. She studied his profile, his firm chin and sensitive mouth, smiling now at something his mother had said. His eyebrows and long sweeping eyelashes were much darker than she'd ever imagined them to be, contrasting with his sunshine-yellow hair.

Wasted on a man, she thought. Almost the eyes of a woman, except when they look at me the way they do. I wish he did love me, she thought. Because I could easily love him. Because I already do.

*   *   *

The Monday club for disabled children was just ending as Leigh entered the centre next morning just before lunch. Pauline was talking earnestly to one of the parents, a thin woman in a vinyl coat. Daphne was having a discussion with the physiotherapist, but she moved away when she saw Leigh approaching.

'Leigh—I wanted to catch you—a phone call. You're not going home just yet, are you?'

'Not yet. I just called in to write up the cards before I go home for lunch.'

'How's your mother?'

Leigh followed Daphne into their office, and sat at her desk. Daphne pulled up a chair. She was wearing a mushroom-coloured pinafore dress and a brown jumper with shapeless sleeves, and looked her usual drab self. She peered shrewdly at Leigh through her gold-rimmed spectacles.

'My mother's fine, thank you. We had quite an—eventful weekend, and it did wear her out a little, but I do think she may be coming to the Tuesday club tomorrow afternoon. I tried to persuade her, but it was after seeing Mrs Chr—Clark—er—yesterday that did it . . .

She tailed off, stuttering, suddenly aware that she was creating a web of deceit. She had very nearly said Mrs Christie, but it was far too soon to admit any involvement in that direction. As it was, Daphne was watching her keenly.

'Mrs Clark?' she queried. 'Do I know her?'

'No—she's just a friend of ours. She's badly crippled with osteoarthritis, can hardly walk. I took Mother to see her, and it seemed to do them both good.'

'I'm sure. A nasty thing, arthritis. My

121

mother had it. And I believe Dr Christie's mother has it quite badly.'

Leigh felt a guilty flush creep up her cheeks. She fiddled with her files. 'Is that so? You said something about a phone call.'

'That's right. Mrs Rochelle, Manor Square. Newish family. I think Carol was due to visit, then she went off with her wretched hypertension. Mrs Rochelle seemed very worried about her little boy. She says no one's visited her for about a year. Well, of course, that isn't our fault—she's only been in Mossgate for about four months. I spoke to Adam, and he's seen the child a couple of times. He did wonder if there was something wrong with him, but couldn't put his finger on it. The child apparently had a very traumatic birth, but it seems the mother wasn't told all the details. He said if you want to know more there's a report in his medical file which you can read. Put you in the picture, as it were, give you an idea of the problem.'

'If she's so worried, this Mrs Rochelle,' Leigh said, 'why doesn't she take him to see Adam again? I'm not a doctor.'

'The way I see it, Leigh, she just wants to talk, get it off her chest. She may say more to you than to a man.'

Mrs Fletcher hasn't, thought Leigh. 'Do you think it's urgent?' she asked.

'It probably isn't, but we'd better not take that risk. Call in some time this week, if you can.'

'I might be able to fit it in this afternoon. I'll see.' Leigh opened her desk file and flipped through the cards for the Rochelle child. As she found it, and looked up to say something to Daphne, the door opened and Adam walked in. Leigh felt a tell-tale flush creep up her cheeks, and turned away. This would never do, this dreadful lack of control whenever he was around.

But he only glanced at her and smiled, and crossed to Daphne's desk.

'About the Luke Middleton case conference, Daphne, at two o'clock. I'm not sure I can make it on time. I tried to get a social worker, to explain, but no go. And I don't think I'm an important cog in the wheel, anyway. Dr Raybould was on duty at the Queen Anne when the child was brought in, and the family has never visited here. Do you think you could put that over for me, if I can't get there in time? I've got an urgent psychiatric visit to make.'

Daphne listened to his long explanation, nodding at intervals.

'I'll tell them, Adam. I don't expect Paul Deeley will be very happy. But I will tell them what you've said.'

'Thanks, Daphne. I'll do my best to be there.' Adam hurried from the room, and Leigh kept her head averted, so she didn't notice whether he looked at her or not.

Daphne turned towards her.

'This would have been your case, Leigh, in the ordinary way of things. A baby battering— a nasty case, but the child is recovering, and will go into care until something's sorted out. It happened while Carol was still here, so it fell to me when Maureen zipped off ill. And these things usually drag on for a long time, so I'd better carry on with it, don't you think?'

'Since I'm temporary, it would be easier, I suppose,' Leigh agreed. Privately, she was relieved. After Sunday's revelations by Grace Christie, the fewer the chances of contact between herself and Adam the better. It would give her time to get her feelings in order. Just the sight and sound of him set her pulses tingling with desire. It had to be love, because she'd never felt like this before. It was like being on a rollercoaster, and she was afraid she might fall off.

*   *   *

Evelyn had surprised Leigh by having the lunch all ready by the time she got home. She was feeling very pleased with herself, and kept referring to the meal Grace Christie had given them on Sunday.

'I don't know whether she does any cooking,' she said, as they sat down to eat, 'because she has that Mrs Dunn, but I don't expect she's there all the time.'

'You seemed to get on with Mrs Christie,' remarked Leigh.

'I didn't like her much at first. She seemed rather autocratic, if you know what I mean—a bit bossy. I suppose she's been used to having her own way. Did you like her, Leigh?'

'Not at first, I'm afraid. But we got talking, and I think I understand her more now. She seems very protective of Adam.'

'I wonder why? Adam seems to be very fond of you.'

'Mother, the visit was for your benefit, not mine. And I'm glad to see it worked—seeing Mrs Christie, I mean. She's a very positive thinker, isn't she?'

Evelyn conceded this. 'It wasn't just her influence, though. I've been thinking for some time that I should try to be more independent, ever since Kate went. You're not going to be here forever, and I don't want to be an inconvenience to people for the rest of my life.'

'Mother, you're not—'

'I've decided I don't want to go to Oxford. It's about time their lives were their own. And the way I've succeeded with this meal has shown me I shan't need to depend on people much longer. So you can go off and marry your nice doctor, or Colin, or whoever—'

'I have no intention of marrying anyone just yet, Mother. And Colin is just a friend.'

Evelyn gave her a long look but said

nothing. Together they took the plates into the kitchen.

'You'd better be getting back,' said Evelyn. I'll do these.' And she was smiling as Leigh went down the path.

*   *   *

The Rochelles lived in a smart detached house in Manor Square, a crescent that joined Banbury Road at each end, curving away around the park. The drive to the house was lined with an orange-berried cotoneaster hedge on one side, with mock orange and a beautiful red-berried rowan tree on the other. In between was fuchsia and bright scarlet berberis.

Mrs Rochelle stood in the doorway as Leigh approached. She had obviously seen her arrive. She was tall and slim, and wore a midnight-blue dress, belted with a lime-green sash.

'You're the health visitor? You look very young.' She wasn't very old herself, and Leigh felt sure she'd seen her somewhere before. She didn't comment on her own youth, but followed her into a huge drawing-room, the walls of which were almost covered by large modem paintings and sketches, mostly pen-and-wash, and some misty-looking water-colours.

'I didn't expect you to come so soon,' said

126

Mrs Rochelle. Leigh was racking her memory to place her.

'I was already planning to visit along here,' she said, taking the card from her bag. 'I believe you're rather worried about—' she glanced at the card '—Harry.' Her eyes took in the details quickly. Harry Percival Rochelle, age almost three. Mother—Jodie Marina. Maiden name Matlock. Jodie Matlock! The television presenter! Leigh remembered now. A late-night programme, current events, social problems, controversial cases . . . *The Other Side.* That was it! *The Other Side.* Presented by Jodie Matlock.

She didn't look much different, thought Leigh, even without all that theatre make-up. She had very attractive eyes, a sort of smoky colour, and reddish-blonde hair. That was why I didn't recognise her straight away, thought Leigh. She's got her hair tied back and no lipstick on.

'He's in his room,' said Mrs Rochelle. 'Do you mind if we talk first?'

'Not at all. That might be better.'

'You see, there's really nothing to see,' explained Mrs Rochelle. 'He looks normal, he doesn't misbehave when I take him out, he sleeps well, he eats well.' She gave a little laugh. 'You'll be wondering next why I've asked you to call.'

'He certainly does sound like a perfect child, Mrs Rochelle. There must be hundreds of mothers who'd love a child like Harry.'

Mrs Rochelle sighed. 'Well, that's what's wrong. He's too good! My sister came to stay last week, and brought her four-year-old daughter. It was that that made me decide to do something. I don't think he's normal, Miss—?'

'Rochester. Leigh Rochester.'

'Leigh—what a pretty name. I'm—Jodie.'

Leigh smiled. 'Yes, I knew that. I've seen you on television.'

'Yes. Well, what should I do?'

'Have you spoken to your doctor? Dr Christie?'

'Not specifically about his being too good. That would have sounded silly. I wondered if he might be deaf. He doesn't talk, you see. Although he did start to talk, as a baby— babbled a lot, then he stopped. That's why I thought he might be deaf. But he doesn't act like a deaf child. He starts at noises, you see. He hears them. But he doesn't seem to hear us speak to him. And he started to rub his ear. I thought he might have an ear infection.'

'And did he?'

Jodie looked embarrassed. 'Sort of. An irritation. He'd pushed a bead into it. I can't think where he got the bead from, unless it was Isobel. She's a girl who comes to help out, but she's very young. Willing, but not very bright, I'm afraid.'

'Any problem getting the bead out?'

128

'Dr Christie took it out, of course. He was surprised that Harry hadn't made more fuss about it. He said it must have been quite painful. But he never cried. He never does cry! He doesn't seem to feel pain at all.' Jodie's lovely eyes were full of distress.

'That's very strange,' murmured Leigh. There was a condition in which pain was never felt, but the children were usually otherwise normal. This child didn't appear to be normal at all!

'I had to take Harry to see Dr Christie a few days later,' Jodie went on. 'I'd been putting a bit of a wave in my hair, and he just came and picked up the hot curling tongs without any warning. He just stood there, holding them— by the curling ends, not the handle. When I grabbed them from him, he seemed most surprised to see the palm of his hand all red and raw.'

'He must have cried then!' exclaimed Leigh.

'Not a sound. I rushed him to Dr Christie, but I'd put cold water on it first, and he dressed it, and it healed remarkably quickly.'

'I'm not surprised you're worried about him—he could really harm himself and not be aware of it.'

Jodie nodded. 'If you take all these things singly, they don't sound so bad. But put them all together—like the way he clings to the radiators, doesn't like the cold, doesn't respond when we talk to him, and the way . . .

the way—it's almost as if we aren't there, if you know what I mean.'

'He doesn't talk at all?' asked Leigh.

'He should, shouldn't he? He's almost three. In December. There's just one word he says, and it isn't a proper word—"pother". It's all he ever says. He calls everything "pother". Perhaps it does mean something. But I don't know where he's heard it. I think he's made it up.'

'Does he play with his toys?'

'Drags them around with him. He gets attached to something, won't be parted from it. He does repetitive things—spins wheels for hours, that sort of thing. The only time he does get upset is when we try to take him away from what he's doing. Then he screams. We don't do it any more.'

Leigh stood up. 'May I see him now?'

'Sure. He's in the nursery with Isobel. He won't let her play with him—ignores her most of the time. He won't look at you. But I have to have someone with him, to keep an eye on him.'

'Of course.'

As they walked up the thickly carpeted stairs, Leigh was recalling lectures they'd been given during training. Lack of response, no eye contact, repetitive actions, dislike of cold—

They reached the landing. 'Does he object when you pick him up?' she asked.

'He hates to be picked up. He hates contact

130

of any sort. Even as a baby he never put up his arms as other babies do.'

They reached a door painted pale blue. 'Why didn't you tell Dr Christie all this?' asked Leigh.

'I've told you, it was only last week I began to see what was wrong. This is the nursery.'

Jodie pushed open the door and they went inside. A plump girl with mousey hair in a plait looked up as they entered. The child sitting in the middle of the floor made no response. He was busy twirling the wheels on a toy car. Isobel sat on the broad window-seat and watched him.

'Harry, darling, Mummy's here,' called Jodie. He carried on twirling. She put her hands around him to pick him up, but he squirmed away, and moved to another patch of carpet. Leigh watched all this, an idea forming in her mind.

'You see?' said Jodie. Isobel got up.

'Shall I put him down for his nap, Mrs Rochelle?' she asked.

'Yes, please, Isobel.' She patted Harry on his little blond head.

'Pother,' said Harry, watching the wheels go round.

Jodie and Leigh went downstairs. At the bottom, Jodie said, 'I was right, wasn't I? He's mentally handicapped.'

'Mrs Rochelle, it's not my place to diagnose,' said Leigh. 'I suppose there's a

131

chance he may be mentally handicapped, but, putting all those signs and symptoms together, the ones you've told me, leads me to think it may well be something else.'

'What could it be? You must tell me!'

'I think you ought to take him to see a paediatrician. Dr Christie will refer you.'

'You know what it is! Why won't you tell me?' begged Jodie.

'Because it isn't my place to. It's just an idea I have.'

'I shan't sleep tonight if you don't tell me what you think. And how can you expect me to present a show tonight with this on my mind?'

Leigh sighed. 'I may be wrong, but I have a feeling he may be autistic.'

'Autistic—I've heard of that. Can it be cured?'

'I can't tell you any more. You need an expert. I'm not even sure—it was just a guess.'

'An educated guess, I'm sure. Thank you, Leigh, for telling me. I shan't forget you. Oh, I'm such a bad hostess, I never offered you a drink.'

'Thank you, but I have to go now,' said Leigh. 'More visits.'

She walked down the wide drive, aware that Jodie Matlock was standing at the window, watching her. She was beginning to doubt the wisdom of telling her what she thought, but she had felt quite sure of her diagnosis. And it was part of her job to reassure mothers as well as their children, after all. She liked to think she'd reassured Jodie Matlock.

*   *   *

By the time she'd seen all her other families, and was driving back to the centre, some of her doubts and misgivings had returned. Supposing it wasn't autism after all, but some brain disease? Daphne had said the child had had a traumatic birth. Some birth injury? What had been his Apgar score? She'd had no right to rush out with that diagnosis without checking his birth details first. It was unforgivable. Was it too late to check now?

She hurried into the centre and across to the reception desk. The girls all looked very busy, and the one she spoke to replied irritably that they were too busy to find medical records for her, why didn't she look for them herself?

Shrugging, Leigh went into the office and flipped through the Rs. Raybould, Reckitt, Richards, Robbins—Rochelle— The folder next to the Rochelles was headed 'Evelyn May Rochester'. Her heart started to pound. Why hadn't she thought of this before? This was the only way she would ever know the truth! Nonchalantly she took it out of the rack and left the office.

Her own office was deserted. Feeling guilty but excited, she pulled out the cards, turning quickly back to the dates of ten years ago. And here it was: Evelyn's visit to the centre. The doctor had abbreviated most of his findings, but she understood them: 'c/o headaches. ?Menopause. ?Migraine. BP 140/85. ?further investigations'.

But nothing had been done! How could this doctor have failed to see what was wrong? Then her vision seemed to blur as she read the doctor's signature. It was very clear. A. Christie.

CHAPTER EIGHT

Adrenalin surged through Leigh's body as she realised what she was looking at. After ten years, she now knew who had been that locum, the young, inexperienced locum who had misdiagnosed her mother's illness. But Adam Christie! It just couldn't be true! From what she had seen of him during the short time she had been here, he wasn't the sort to fob off patients with easy diagnoses, to make easy promises and not carry them out. She looked again at his report. An R in a circle. If that meant Refer—and of course it might mean something else—then he must have referred her mother to someone. Yet she hadn't seen anyone, and not even any record in her hospital file that she'd been given an appointment to see anyone. What could have

134

happened?

The only conclusion she could come to was that the R in a circle meant something other than Refer, and he hadn't intended to refer Evelyn at all. So why 'further investigations'? In the future, no doubt, if she didn't improve.

Oh, Adam, she thought, this doesn't seem like you at all. You're kind, conscientious, caring—I've seen all that. Yet what I'm looking at now is in black and white and can't be denied. You were here ten years ago—and you must have been very young, she thought distractedly, no more than twenty-four or -five. And inexperienced. Possibly just getting over being jilted? There's no point in making excuses for him, she insisted. I can't let this rest now I've seen it. I have to tell him, listen to his side of the case. There has to be a good reason for what he did, for delaying expert advice. But it all looks pretty damning, she sighed.

Still feeling numb with shock, she pushed the cards back into the envelope and picked up her bag. She would go and see him right away, while it was all fresh in her mind. She left the office and walked determinedly across to the reception window. The clerks all looked very busy. For a few seconds her nerve almost failed her. It would be so much easier to just leave the cards here, go away, never mention what she'd seen. She half turned away.

One of the girls came towards the window,

smiling. She reached out for the file Leigh was holding.

'Finished with it?' She glanced at it. 'Didn't you say Rochelle? This is Rochester.' She stared curiously at her.

'Yes—yes, I know. I took the wrong one by mistake. I was in a hurry, not used to your filing system—' Leigh stammered.

'Why didn't you bring it back straight away? Dr Christie's been looking for this. We couldn't imagine who'd got it.'

'Dr Christie?' echoed Leigh. 'Is he still here?'

'Oh, no, he's gone now. He was in a hurry—going to Edinburgh for a medical conference.'

'Edinburgh? For how long?' The girl seemed to be watching her suspiciously, so Leigh gave her a disarming smile. 'It's just that I was hoping to see him—about a patient. Yes, the Rochelle child. When will he be back?'

'Thursday. You still want the Rochelle file?'

'Oh—well, not yet, I suppose. I'll look at it before Thursday.'

'Afternoon. He'll be here in the afternoon,' said the girl.

Thursday. Two whole days without him. Two whole days to keep this revelation to herself. Two days in which to change her mind. No, she mustn't back down. She had to be honest with herself, and with Adam, if there was ever going to be any future in their relationship.

Don't hurt him, Grace Christie had warned her. Don't let him down. Leigh sighed. Telling Adam this would embarrass him, in the least. She'd have to be very tactful about it. Supposing he'd forgotten all about her mother's visit? Ten years was a long time. Perhaps it might be better to—

'Is that all, Miss Rochester?' The receptionist's voice broke in on her thoughts.

'Oh—yes, thank you. I'll look at the Rochelle file tomorrow.' She smiled cheerfully at her and left the centre.

Once in her car she sat looking unseeing in front of her. For five years she had wondered who that locum had been, what sort of a person he was—but not obsessively, although it could have been, since it had crossed her mind many times that one day she might know—and now she did know, and she wished she didn't. Of all the people it could have been, why did it have to be Adam? Even that wouldn't have been such a problem if she hadn't felt emotionally involved with him. Now, if she told him, would it destroy everything between them? Yet her conscience wouldn't allow her to stay silent.

'Oh, God, this is awful!' she groaned aloud. 'And there's no one I can ask for advice.'

Releasing a huge, desperate sigh, she started her car and drove carefully out of the car park. She felt confused and disillusioned.

'Had a good day?' Evelyn called out from

the kitchen, as soon as Leigh had closed the front door. Leigh could hear her stirring a pot of tea. She hung up her coat, and left her bag on the hall table.

'A very busy day,' she admitted, watching her mother gamely attempting the tasks other people did without thinking. Impulsively she put her arms around her and kissed her.

'Now what do you want?' asked Evelyn gruffly. She had never been a very demonstrative person.

'Nothing.' Leigh realised she had to keep her discovery from her mother. Evelyn seemed to be improving, since yesterday's outing. She was more cheerful. There was no sense in raking up old embers.

'Let's go to the pictures tonight,' she suggested.

'You know the nearest cinema's in the city centre,' said Evelyn, pouring the tea with her good hand. 'Slice of cherry cake?'

'Mmm! Looks like home-made.'

'It is. I made it this afternoon.'

They sat companionably at the kitchen table. Leigh couldn't get over the fact that she'd had a tremendous shock, yet here she was, chatting to her mother, picking cake crumbs from her plate, as though everything were just the same. Evelyn was talking about a radio play she'd heard, but all Leigh could see was Adam's endearing face, his summer-blue eyes, that disarming mouth that would rouse

138

her to such passion. How could he react when she revealed her discovery? She would have to admit she'd read her mother's medical file, and he'd probably be— She took a quick breath. Her mother's file. What had the girl said? Dr Christie wanted it, and they'd looked everywhere for it. Why? Her mother hadn't been to see a doctor lately, she wasn't being referred anywhere, no new treatment was being started. Why should Adam want to look at her mother's file?

Her fingers anxiously crushed a small piece of cake into crumbs.

'I suppose it was predictable—' Her mother broke off, and stared at Leigh. 'Is something wrong, Leigh? You seem distracted.'

Leigh tore her thoughts back to the present, and smiled at her mother.

'Eh? Sorry—I was miles away. Very rude of me. Carry on. He was crossing the bridge.'

Evelyn didn't answer. She frowned. 'What's happened?'

'Nothing!' Leigh answered too quickly, she knew. 'Nothing's wrong. I'm just a bit tired, that's all.'

'Not much point in going to the pictures, then. You'll probably fall asleep.'

'No, I think it would be a good idea.'

'A distraction, you mean.' Sometimes her mother was too perceptive.

'No, just a contrast with health centres, and patients. And doctors,' Leigh added, without thinking.

'It's Adam, isn't it?'

'Mother, there's nothing wrong!'

'I knew there was something as soon as you stepped through the door. I could tell.'

It had been a mistake, being demonstrative, thought Leigh. She should have behaved as she always did.

'Mother, you're imagining things!' She tried to laugh it off.

Her mother looked stubborn. 'Say what you like, there's something wrong. You can't hide it from me.'

Leigh didn't answer. The urge to tell her mother was strong, so she said nothing. Evelyn collected the cups and plates and carefully carried them to the sink.

'I'll wash them,' said Leigh. 'Shall we go and have a meal before we go to the pictures? Go and look in the paper, tell me what you'd like to see, and we'll go to that place that's down in a cellar—you remember, where they play the piano?'

'In Maryann Street,' Evelyn added, nodding. 'Less chance of being able to talk, I suppose.' She cast Leigh a shrewd glance.

'That wasn't why I suggested it,' said Leigh, crossing her fingers behind her back.

'I don't think I feel like going out,' said Evelyn. 'Yesterday tired me out, I think. Perhaps we could go later in the week. Thursday?'

'I've got a rehearsal on Thursday,' said Leigh. Adam comes back on Thursday, she thought. And I shall have to tell him.

'Perhaps Wednesday, then.'

'Perhaps.' But the suggestion was made half-heartedly, and so was Leigh's response. The truth was, neither of them really wanted to go out, but Leigh felt she needed some distraction from the constant feeling of apprehension which clouded her thoughts. If only she could forget about it until Thursday!

'Perhaps I'll get an early night,' she said, trying to sound casual. 'I'll have a long soak and read in bed.'

'It won't help, you know,' said her mother, putting the rest of the cake in a tin. 'Why don't you want to talk about it?'

'Mother, you're the giddy limit! You're like a dog with a bone—you won't let go. I've told you—'

'You haven't told me the truth. But I can't force you, so let's forget it.'

I wish I could, thought Leigh. Her mother looked sad and disappointed as she gathered up the tablecloth, and Leigh felt a twinge of guilt. She had always confided in her mother, had always felt close to her. Were they drifting apart? Those seven years away couldn't have helped. Perhaps she could compromise ...

'You're right, of course, Mother,' she said, crossing to the sink and running water into the bowl. Evelyn didn't answer, but Leigh heard a

141

chair creak as she sat down.

'It is to do with Adam,' Leigh went on, 'and what his mother told me.'

'I did wonder. You know, Leigh, you seemed different during the drive back from Stow. Did she say something to upset you?'

No, thought Leigh. But Adam kissed me, and that was an upset of quite a different sort. She turned to face her mother.

'Not really. It was just—well, Mrs Christie seemed to have the wrong idea about Adam and me.'

Evelyn gave her a shrewd glance. 'How wrong?'

'She felt it was necessary that I should know about his ex-fiancée from a good many years ago.'

Evelyn nodded. 'I have to admit, I did think it strange that someone like Adam, of Adam's age, should still be single.' She spoke defensively. 'Well, anyone would, wouldn't they? He's very attractive, and extremely eligible.'

'She jilted him and went to Africa. And she's just returned,' Leigh told her.

'And you think he may still be carrying a torch for her?'

'I can't possibly know that. Mrs Christie feels sure he's well over it now. But it could still be the reason he's been so reluctant to commit himself again.'

'And Grace Christie told you because she

142

sensed that you're in love with him.'

Colour flooded Leigh's cheeks. 'No, Mother. She thought he might be in love with me, and she doesn't want to see him hurt again. That's why she told me.'

'But she guessed correctly, didn't she? You are in love with Adam.'

'I don't know—I hardly know him.'

Evelyn smiled. 'That's irrelevant. I knew I'd fallen in love with your father the first time I set eyes on him. It can happen that way, you know.'

Leigh thought of that day in the Square at Stow, the blueness of Adam's eyes as he'd looked at her, the way his long, sensitive hands had massaged the man's chest, hands that she now realised she'd wanted to touch her, even then.

She looked at her mother. 'Yes, you're right—I do love him. But that isn't enough, is it? He has to fall in love with me too. And I'm not sure he will. Perhaps he's not ready. Perhaps it's not the right time.'

'Is there ever a right time to fall in love?' asked Evelyn softly.

*   *   *

Leigh managed to get through the next day without causing comment on her lack of concentration. She pored over the Rochelle file, reading the details of Harry's birth. A

143

difficult breech delivery, by all accounts, and the baby had been very shocked, with a low Apgar score. He'd recovered, and there had been no apparent problems.

Low Apgar score, Leigh had mused. This was the index used to record the physical state of a baby immediately after birth. She recalled a lecture given by an eminent child specialist when she was a student health visitor. In his experience, every child born with a low Apgar score suffered some sort of problem later on.

Certainly true in this case, Leigh privately agreed. Perhaps not in every case.

I think I suggested the correct diagnosis, she thought again. There could have been minimal brain damage in Harry Rochelle—a possible cause of autism. This official support for her theory gave her increased confidence, and she began to feel more capable of dealing with Adam when he came back.

*   *   *

On Wednesday morning she found a letter on the mat in unfamiliar writing. She tore it open. The address was St Edward's Drive, Stow-on-the-Wold.

> Dear Miss Rochester,
> I must apologise for not writing sooner, but my husband's illness was so unexpected it threw me out of my usual

routine. I really must thank you from the bottom of my heart for the prompt way in which you revived my husband when he had his heart attack. Without you and Dr Christie, I'm sure he would have died. Gerald is out of hospital now, and doing very well. We are both very grateful to you, and if ever you come to Stow again we would like to see you. We are just off the Oddington Road.

Words are very inadequate to say what we feel. Thank you again,
Margaret Keith

Leigh smiled and refolded the letter. Nice to feel appreciated, even though it reminded her of that day in Stow, and her first meeting with Adam. Such a short time ago, yet such a lot had happened. So many new people had come into her life, both hers and her mother's.

Yesterday Evelyn had been persuaded to go along to the Tuesday club. She'd worn her deep blue jersey dress and her pearls, and had tried to hide her misgivings. Afterwards Leigh had brought her home quite a different person, laughing, confident, and full of praise for Graham Scott and the way he organised the group without apparently doing so.

'Oh, yes,' she had told Leigh, 'of course I'm going again next week. You try and keep me away!' She had given her a sidelong glance. 'Of course, I was very keen on the idea from the start, if you remember.'

Leigh had hidden a smile. 'Of course you were, Mother.'

The hours at the centre seemed to drag. Leigh was glad to be busy with clinics and visiting. She'd called in on Pamela Varley for a few minutes, and had been relieved to see the woman, still pale, but obviously happier with the situation, and willing to accept Leigh's explanation. She'd talked to her husband, and he was being more supportive than she'd expected. Healthwise she wasn't really well yet, a lot of nausea and sickness, but psychologically . . .

Leigh was glad someone's problems were being sorted out! Not Mrs Fletcher's, it seemed. Leigh met her in the street on Wednesday afternoon, and Susan seemed just as tense and anxious as before—now she thought she had pleurisy!

Leigh tried to question her, but it was impossible in a busy street, with Kim hopping from foot to foot.

She went back to her car. Headaches, indigestion, pleurisy. What was *really* wrong? she thought.

*   *   *

Leigh went into the centre on Thursday feeling tense and apprehensive. She had a busy day ahead, with the baby clinic during the morning, and visits during the afternoon. And she had to fit in Adam somewhere. The thought made her pulses race and her stomach churn.

At nine-fifteen the phone rang. Daphne answered it, and her face changed as she listened.

'Is there no one else, Pauline? You know how busy we are. Yes, of course you'll have to go with him. I'm sure we'll manage. Don't fuss, Pauline! I'm sure everything will be all right. Yes, see you tomorrow. Don't worry!'

Leigh glanced at her. She'd wondered why Pauline was so late. 'Is Pauline ill?' she asked.

'No—thank goodness. It's her father. He's quite elderly and not very good on his pins, and he's got an appointment at the Queen Anne this lunchtime—his stomach, by all accounts—and Pauline's aunt was going to take him. Now she's gone down with flu, so Pauline has to go.'

'At least she's not ill,' Leigh said optimistically.

'True—but who's going to give her talk at the maternity hospital this afternoon?' Daphne pointed out. 'I can't, I've got health education at Mossgate Comprehensive. I don't suppose you—'

'Well, I've got nothing urgent on, I suppose—' Leigh began.

'Good. That's solved, then. It's immunisation, two-thirty to four. You'll find all the visual aids and things in the antenatal room at the hospital.'

Leigh sighed, and put the cards she'd selected back in the filing cabinet. She would have to do them tomorrow.

Arriving back from lunch, she went straight to the reception window. The girl who had been so suspicious of her on Monday gave her a beaming smile.

'Can I help you, Miss Rochester?'

'Will you give me a buzz as soon as Dr Christie arrives? Only I have to leave before quarter-past two.'

The girl stared at her. 'Dr Christie? Isn't he away? Oh, wait a minute—that's right, he's got a surgery at three. Last appointment four-thirty.'

Leigh sighed with relief. 'That's fine. I should be back by then. I'll see him when he's finished.'

'Shall I tell him?' asked the girl.

'Oh—no, it's all right.' Leigh gave her a brief smile and went along to her office. Continually postponing the task was making things very difficult indeed!

She arrived at the hospital to find the antenatal room already in use by one of the anaesthetists, who was demonstrating pain-relief techniques. Leigh went to find the outpatients sister, who seemed surprised at her query.

'Two-thirty? But didn't you know? The

148

other health visitor, the one who usually comes, agreed to the change of time.'

'Miss Morris,' said Leigh. 'I'm standing in for her today.'

'She should have told you. This was the only time Dr Phillips had free, two till three. Miss Morris agreed to come three to four-thirty. I'm afraid you'll just have to wait until he's finished.' Sister smiled. 'He may finish early.'

He won't, thought Leigh crossly. And he didn't. And by the time she'd talked about the various diseases prevented by immunisation, and answered hundreds of questions, it was ten to five. By the time she'd put away the visual aids and rushed back to the clinic, it was ten past five, and, of course, Adam had gone. Leigh felt like bursting into tears of frustration. But she forced a smile.

'He'll be in first thing in the morning,' said the receptionist cheerfully. 'Will that do?'

No, thought Leigh, it won't. She'd have to tell him tonight, after the rehearsal. She turned away from the window.

'Oh, Miss Rochester,' called the girl, 'I nearly forgot. There was a phone call for you. It went through to Dr Christie by mistake. I—we—thought he said *Mrs* Rochester.'

'A man?'

'Yes. He wouldn't give his name. He spoke to Dr Christie. You'll have to ask him tomorrow. It didn't sound urgent.'

'Yes, I'll do that.' A man? Leigh's heart sank. Could it have been Colin?

*   *   *

Leigh sat down with her mother to eat cheese-filled jacket potatoes and salad. Evelyn talked easily about her ideas for refurbishing the bathroom. Leigh didn't feel like talking, so she just nodded and agreed. When it was time, she went up and changed into her dark green cords, a green and gold patterned overshirt over a gold cotton jumper. She had always felt green was a lucky colour for her, and she needed luck tonight.

Tonight was the first time she'd arrived alone, and her heart was beating like a sledge-hammer as she walked through the swing doors to the hall. She wasn't late, but already most of them were there. She could see Adam, turned away from her, bent attentively towards Sarah. Sarah was looking at him with big doe eyes, her lips slightly apart as she listened, and Leigh was surprised by the depth of her emotion as she watched them. Jealousy? Jealousy was a sign of insecurity. Surely there was nothing between Sarah and Adam?

Stop it! she told herself. It's no one and Adam. For the first time, she wondered what Fenella had looked like. Like Sarah, perhaps?

Adam turned as she approached, and a slow smile spread over his face. His blue eyes held

150

hers for a long moment, and there was an expression in them she thought she understood. Her heart seemed to be galloping away with her.

'Leigh, come and sit here.' Sarah gave Leigh a slight smile and went over to Roger, who was deciding what was to be rehearsed that evening. Leigh sat next to Adam.

'You've been away,' she said. She almost added, I've missed you, but she didn't want him to see her vulnerability.

'I was in Edinburgh, at a conference,' he told her.

'I wanted to see you.' She held her breath. His gaze didn't leave her face. Perhaps she'd phrased it wrongly.

'I wanted to see you.' She had! And now there was no stopping of her madly beating heart. She was sure Adam must be able to hear it. And this utter lack of control when he was near her was going to make things very difficult when she told him what she'd discovered. She licked her lips.

'Mine was a professional matter,' she said, trying not to look into his forget-me-not eyes. Yet where else was she to look, except at his kissable lips? And then she couldn't help remembering . . .

'Oh.' There was the beginning of a smile on his mouth. 'Mine wasn't.'

She wished he wouldn't look at her like that—at least, not here. It made her want to throw caution to the winds, to fling her arms around his neck, to tell him she loved him, to kiss him and kiss him and kiss . . .

'Right, are we ready?' Roger turned to face them all. His gaze rested for a while on Leigh, and she went pink, feeling he had read her thoughts. 'Have you managed to read the play yet, Leigh?' he asked.

'Well, most of it—'

'Yes, I know—don't tell me, you've been very busy. Well, I hope you've read the end, because that's what we're doing tonight—the reconciliation between Rupert and Celia. On stage, please.'

Leigh suddenly realised he meant her. She jumped up, grabbing her book from her bag. Golly, she hadn't read this far! What did it entail? She soon found out.

Celia, hurt and angry by Rupert's defection to Amanda, was at first unwilling to accept his apologies. She stood with her back to him, gazing through a side-window.

Leigh heard him come up behind her. She had to tell herself it was Rupert, not Adam, and that she wasn't Leigh, but her skin still tingled when he gently laid his fingers on her neck.

'It's too late, Rupert,' she cried in anguish— and found that she meant it. It would be too late, once he knew what she'd seen. He wouldn't trust her, nor love her, after that.

His hand stroked her cheek, and she

152

shivered.

'It's not too late. Celia—look at me!' He turned her to face him. 'We loved each other once,' he said harshly. 'You can't deny it. How can you let someone like Amanda come between us?'

'You put her between us!' Her eyes glittered with anger.

'Amanda's nothing to me—nothing! Won't you believe me?'

'I've tried—oh, I've tried—' And suddenly she was in his arms and he was kissing her passionately. And it was Sunday in Stow all over again. Standing in the golden autumn sunshine, just the two of them and no one else in the whole wide world. Already she could feel herself responding, and trying not to, but her senses were swimming, she couldn't resist . . .

'Adam,' came Roger's voice, 'are you sure that kiss isn't rather premature?'

They slowly drew apart, and Adam looked into her darkened hazel eyes. 'Oh, no, Roger,' he said, without taking his gaze from her face, 'I think that's just about the most perfect time for a kiss.'

Leigh couldn't help the delicious tremble that ran through her.

'Well,' said Roger, a bit huffily, 'you're interpreting the part. I'll leave it to you. I must say, it looked good. Carry on.'

Leigh suddenly realised her knees were

trembling. She sank into the nearest chair, relieved that there were to be no more romantic scenes until the very end.

After the tea-break there was a long scene between Mark and Sarah, another scene with Diane, and finally the very last scene—Rupert and Celia.

Leigh faced Adam on the stage. She was determined not to let her true feelings show this time.

'I'm sorry I misunderstood, Rupert,' she said.

He took her hands. 'I'm afraid I didn't explain it very well. It was really a storm in a teacup, you know.'

'Yes, I realise that now.'

He gently lifted her chin and looked at her. She tried to will her heart to behave itself, but it was running a race of its own, and she couldn't stop it. And when he finally embraced her she rested against him for all the world as if she belonged there.

The others clapped. It was over for the night. Much later, they stood outside the hall. Leigh was trembling with anxiety.

'Are you cold?' Adam asked solicitously. He didn't seem in a hurry to leave.

'No—it's just— Adam, there's something I have to tell you. Something I must know.'

'Something you must know?'

The glow from the door lantern turned his hair to gold, and cast shadows over his face.

His eyes seemed to glisten. Leigh swallowed. Her throat felt tight.

'Adam, when I talked to your mother on Sunday, she told me—about the girl you were once engaged to—' Oh, hell, why couldn't she say the words she wanted to, the awful, accusing words that had to be said?

'Fenella? But that was years ago.'

'She's come back from Africa, hasn't she?'

'So I believe. But why should it concern any of us?' He lifted her chin with a forefinger, just as he had in the play. 'Leigh, I can't imagine why you're worried about Fenella. It was all over and done with a long, long time ago. To be honest, I haven't thought about her for years.'

He looked deep into her eyes, into the dark pupils, wide in the tawny irises. 'Leigh, I haven't thought about her, and I don't intend to start now. I don't need to think of her, because there's someone else who takes up all my waking thoughts.'

He dropped a kiss lightly on the tip of her nose, and Leigh's heart swelled with emotion. She could hardly breathe. And she knew, in that moment, she could never tell him what she had discovered.

CHAPTER NINE

Leigh tried to tell herself it was self-preservation, but in her heart she knew it was pure cowardice. Her relationship with Adam was still too fragile to risk spoiling it with revelations of apparent professional negligence. She had to trust him!

He did what he felt was right at that time, she kept telling herself as she drove home. I love him, and I trust him. Her mouth still felt the pressure of his lips on hers, the kiss he'd given her after he'd told her about Fenella.

'Has anyone ever told you your lips taste like candy-floss?' he'd murmured. 'I could kiss them forever and ever.' And then he had done precisely that, tasting and touching with his own, one moment soft and tender like the fleeting kiss of a child, the next, eager, passionate and intimate.

It was because of that kiss that she'd completely forgotten to ask him about the phone call. Forgotten about everything except the touch of his lips on hers. The call couldn't have been important, she reasoned as she drove into the garage. It couldn't have been Colin; he would have rung her at home. And if it had been important Adam would surely have told her.

Evelyn heard her come in, and called from

her bedroom. Leigh put her head round the door.

'All right, Mother?'

Evelyn closed her romantic novel and took off her reading glasses. 'Did you have a nice time?'

'Fine, Mother. Do you want anything before I go to bed?'

'No—I wanted to tell you something. Cora rang. She could hardly speak.'

Cora? thought Leigh. Oh, yes, the friend with the cottage in Wales. She'd forgotten about that.

'I'm not going to Wales—Cora's got some virus,' Evelyn went on. 'Still, I wasn't looking forward to it. She can be very bossy, can Cora.'

'Never mind,' said Leigh. 'I expect something else will turn up. Goodnight.'

'Goodnight,' said Evelyn, and turned out the lamp.

*   *   *

Leigh slept restlessly, her dreams full of symbolism—Colin with Daphne, strange people playing violins in a field, herself with a camera trying to photograph a grasshopper that kept jumping away. She woke wondering where Adam had been, and missing him.

During breakfast she told her mother what Adam had said about Fenella, how he never thought about her these days, he only thought about Leigh. Evelyn, obviously hearing wedding bells, seemed greatly relieved.

'He's such a nice young man,' she said happily. 'But you know I still have this feeling I saw him once a long time ago. It must have been the hospital, although he did say—'

'It wasn't at the hospital. He's never worked at the Queen Anne. Do you think you could be mistaken? Memory's a funny thing, the way it works.'

Evelyn shook her head. 'No, I don't think so. I keep seeing his face, the same but younger—he was writing something—saying something— Oh, I do wish I could remember!'

'You're remembering someone else,' Leigh said quickly, getting up. 'Now I really must go. Will you be all right?'

'Oh, yes, I'll be fine. I just wish—'

Leigh left before her mother could start one of her unsuccessful journeys into her memory.

Ironic, thought Leigh, as she drove to the centre. There was a time when I'd have been thrilled that her memory was returning. Now I don't want it to. I don't want her to remember where she saw Adam before. I just want it all forgotten.

*   *   *

Colin rang while Leigh was busy sorting out cards for visiting. Some she had already decided on yesterday, before she had got

158

roped in to do Pauline's talk. She put them aside and flicked through the others. When the phone rang, Daphne was out of the office, and for that Leigh was relieved when she heard his voice.

'Colin, what a surprise! But why are you ringing me here, at the centre? I really have no time to talk just now, and I'm not even sure Daphne will approve of private phone calls.'

He sounded apologetic. 'That's just it, Leigh—I seem to have lost your address and phone number, but I did remember the name of your health centre.'

'In that case I'd better give you my number again, then you can ring me at home when I've got more time.' Feeling she'd been rather curt with him, Leigh added, 'It'll be nice to talk. Have you a pen handy?' She told him the number, waiting for him to write it down.

'I rang the centre yesterday,' Colin went on, sounding rather aggrieved. 'I got put through to some snooty doctor who was really very curt with me—I can't think why. It wasn't my mistake. I did ask for you.'

'Did you leave your name, Colin? Because I didn't get any message that you'd rung.' She didn't, that was true, she consoled herself.

'I can't remember—perhaps I didn't. Does it matter? The man was really quite abrupt when I mentioned your name. Are they all like that in Mossgate? Because if they are you'd be better off back here in Bath.'

159

Leigh smiled to herself. 'They're mostly very nice here. Colin—I really must go, I've got visits to do. Ring me one evening, all right?'

'The point is, are you all right? Do you really want to stay?'

'I have to stay, Colin, and I do like it. Goodbye.'

He started to say something else, but Leigh was firm, replacing the receiver just as Daphne came back.

'Was that Mrs Hall?' she asked. 'I'm expecting her to ring.'

'No, it was a wrong number—the dental clinic.' Leigh shoved the cards in her bag. Pauline came in, looking flustered. Her father had been kept in hospital for some tests, and she was worried about the dog.

'Thanks for doing my talk, Leigh,' she said, shuffling the papers on her desk. 'Did it go all right?'

'It went fine, Pauline. Just fine.' Leigh didn't mention the forgotten revised schedule, and the problems it had caused her—Pauline had enough problems of her own. So she just smiled and left the office.

Adam was just going into his surgery. He caught her eye and gave her a little wave, and a small ripple of ecstasy ran through her. It was just fine, as she'd told Pauline. Everything was fine. God was in His heaven and all was right with the world. Nothing could spoil it now.

160

Crossing the reception area, she glanced at the patients waiting, in case any were families she was planning to visit. The only familiar face she noticed was Jodie Matlock—Mrs Rochelle. She sat alone, lost in thought, and didn't see Leigh.

Leigh was soon caught up in all the mainly minor problems of her families, and the morning flew. Soon she just had one family to visit—three Asian children in Lily Grove. It was almost lunchtime.

The Begums' house, number 53, was identical with all the others in the row of terraced houses. It had a green-painted door, and heavy curtains covered the windows. She knocked on the door, and it seemed to echo in the quiet street. Inside, a baby started to cry.

Leigh glanced at the card in her hand. That would be Zarida, four months old. She had another card for Sucha, a two-year-old boy, and yet another for Lalita, another girl of almost four. Leigh had read the cards quickly before putting them aside yesterday, and was quite relieved to see that Mrs Begum had had an intrauterine contraceptive device inserted. It appeared she'd been very unhappy after the recent birth of another girl, and had decided enough was enough. And, according to Lalita's card, there was another older child of about nine. Another girl, perhaps?

No one seemed to have heard her knock. The baby still cried. She tried again, harder.

Then she heard a child's voice, and a door somewhere banged. The heavy bolts on the front door were finally drawn back, and it was opened a few inches. Leigh, expecting to see Mrs Begum, looked down and saw a little girl dressed in blue satin brocade. She seemed to be about seven or eight.

'What do you want?' she asked, in perfect English.

'Is your mother in? Mrs Begum?'

'Yes. She's resting. I'm Sakina. Come inside, please.'

Leigh followed her through a dim, cluttered room and into another one, where a large electric fire burned brightly, and two small children played on the carpet. Fortunately there was a fire-guard—of sorts!

'Why aren't you at school, Sakina?' she asked the child. Very small for nine, she thought.

'I am helping my mother to look after the baby.' The baby lay on a sofa, sucking at a bottle of what looked like milky tea.

'Where is your mother? I'd like to speak to her.'

'I'll fetch her.'

Sakina disappeared, and Leigh heard her running footsteps on the stairs. Left alone, she was able to check on the children briefly. They seemed healthy enough, the little boy considerably plumper than his sisters. They were dressed well, and played contentedly on the carpet with a plastic truck and a doll with no arms.

Sakina came running in. 'She's coming. She wants to know who you are.'

'I'm Leigh Rochester. I'm a health visitor. And I'm new to the area, so she hasn't seen me before.'

The child called back to her mother, in Punjabi or Hindi, or Gujarati—Leigh wouldn't have known the difference anyway—and it quickly became apparent to her that Mrs Begum didn't speak English. Sakina was quite happy to act as interpreter.

Mrs Begum's face was lined in pain. She sank on to a chair, her hands massaging her stomach.

'Is she ill?' Leigh asked Sakina. The child translated.

'She has a lot of stomach pain, starting in the night.'

'Where is your father? At work?'

'In India, at my uncle's funeral.'

'Does your mother get a lot of stomach pain?' It might be a regular occurrence, thought Leigh. The woman shook her head.

'Never before. Except when she's having a baby,' said Sakina, who was obviously well versed in reproduction. Leigh stared at Mrs Begum, who was bent double every couple of minutes. A baby? Miscarriage? But it couldn't be that. She had a contraceptive coil.

'Sakina—could she be expecting a baby?'

The woman shook her head angrily.

'No,' said Sakina. 'She can't have any more babies now.' Leigh bit her lip, racking her brain for possibilities. The coil wasn't a hundred per cent safe; there was a very slight chance— But she insists she's not pregnant, she thought. That could only mean one thing. She jumped up.

'Sakina, do you have a phone?' The child pointed to it, on a cupboard near the window. 'I must ring the doctor. Will you tell your mother?'

Mrs Begum didn't respond. She sat rocking in pain, only half aware of what was going on around her.

Leigh rang the centre and was put through to Adam. 'Hello, Adam—thank goodness I've found you.'

His voice was strangely cool. 'Is something wrong, Leigh? I'm about to start my visits.'

'I'm at Mrs Begum's house, in Lily Grove. Adam, I'm sure she's heading for a ruptured ectopic. Could you make it your first call?'

'An ectopic pregnancy? Are you sure? She's got a coil in, hasn't she?'

'She has. And, whatever it is, she's in a lot of pain. It looks like an ectopic—I've seen them before.'

'I'm sure you have, but I'd be obliged if you'd leave the diagnosis to me. I'll be there right away. What number?'

Leigh couldn't speak for a moment. Then she said in a small voice, 'Fifty-three.'

The phone at the other end was replaced with a clatter. For a moment Leigh just stood and looked at the receiver in her hand. She felt as though she'd been slapped. Leave the diagnosis to him? Did he doubt her experience, her qualifications? He'd never spoken like this to her before. Why this sudden change in him? It was little more than two hours since he'd waved and smiled at her as she'd left. What could have happened since then?

But there wasn't time to worry about that now. If Mrs Begum had to go to hospital, some arrangements would have to be made for the care of the children. She turned to Sakina.

If your mother has to go into hospital for a while, is there anyone who could look after you and the little ones?'

'But I can look after them. I'm nine. I can make feeds and do shopping.'

'I'm sure you could, but, you see, it would be against the law. And you have to go to school, I'm afraid. Do you like school?'

'Oh, yes.' Sakina frowned in concentration. 'There's my aunty in Selly Oak. She got married in May. She doesn't have any children.'

'Does she have a phone number? Does she speak English?'

'Oh, yes, she's always lived here. This is her

number.' Sakina produced a small notebook from near the phone.

The aunt proved to be quite articulate and sensible, and willing to come to the house to sort something out. Leigh promised to wait there until she arrived, which the woman said would be in around half an hour, depending on the buses.

That's one problem solved, thought Leigh with relief. Just Adam now. And she felt strangely apprehensive, as though she were being hauled on the carpet for some misdemeanour. Could she have done something wrong? If so, she wasn't aware of it. Unless—she'd taken her mother's file and read it! Could that be it? Could someone have told him? And if he had looked at it too, then he would know what she had seen. Her mouth grew suddenly dry. Was there any chance she could still keep quiet about it?

She tried to ignore her disquiet, and turned to Sakina, who was talking in her native language to her mother. Mrs Begum was sweating slightly, and her pulse was rapid.

'Would you get some nightclothes for your mother, Sakina, and put them in a bag? Oh— and soap and toothbrush—'

'She wants me to make her a cup of tea,' said Sakina blithely. 'Would you like one, Miss Lady?'

Despite her alarm, Leigh had to smile. Miss Lady! 'Oh, no, Sakina, your mother mustn't have anything to eat or drink. She may need an operation.' If it is an ectopic she certainly will, she said to herself.

'But she's thirsty.'

'Wet her lips with water. Look, I'll show you.'

They were still doing their best to make poor Mrs Begum comfortable when Adam arrived, and Leigh saw at a glance that something had definitely upset him. Although he was most attentive towards Mrs Begum, and examined her as gently as he could, his lips were compressed, and a small frown creased his forehead.

'You're quite right,' he said to Leigh, as he straightened up. 'I'll get an ambulance right away. I should imagine the tube is on the point of rupture. She'll need immediate surgery.' He glanced quickly at her. 'You haven't given her anything to drink, have you?'

Leigh was astounded. 'Of course not! I am a trained nurse!'

'Yes, of course. I'm sorry.' He crossed to the phone and gave urgent instructions. His voice was firm and authoritative. He turned to her again. 'What about the children? They can't stay here alone. Have you rung Mr Begum yet? He ought to be here.'

Leigh almost flinched at his peremptory tone. 'He's in India, at a funeral. But the children's aunt is coming up from Selly Oak. I said I'd wait until she gets here.'

He nodded, and she noticed a flicker of appreciation in his eyes. But he said nothing, just started to write a letter for the hospital.

'Sakina,' said Leigh, anxious to appear practical, 'I'll come and help you put some things ready for the hospital. Do you have a case? Or a big bag?'

Sakina, happy to show her domestic knowledge, quickly produced a canvas holdall, and Leigh followed her up some narrow, twisting stairs and along a dim corridor to the front bedroom.

They had just zipped up the bag when they heard the approaching sound of the ambulance. They hurried downstairs. Sakina had grown very quiet, and Leigh held her hand encouragingly. The next minutes were rather noisy and chaotic. The smaller children were alarmed by all the strangers in the room, and Lalita began to cry hysterically. The baby started to scream, and Sakina quickly pushed a dummy into her mouth.

'I want to see you when you get back to the centre,' Adam said to Leigh in a low voice, as the ambulance began to draw away. She glanced at him, her hopes rising at his tone. But his expression was still grim, and without further ado he went out to his car and followed the ambulance down the street.

Leigh glanced at her watch. Twenty to one! Surely he didn't expect to see her right now? Mrs Begum was in safe hands, and there would be plenty of time to talk after lunch. A small hand crept into hers and she looked down at Sakina.

'Is she going to die?' whispered the child, and a reluctant tear trickled down her cheek. Impulsively, Leigh bent and hugged her.

'Of course she isn't going to die! She'll have an operation and soon she'll be quite better and home again.'

The child gave a tremulous smile.

'Let's have that cup of tea, shall we?' suggested Leigh, as they closed the front door and went down to the living-room. 'And then your aunt will be here.'

*　　　*　　　*

It was five past one by the time Leigh got back to the centre. There was no sign of Adam, and the place seemed quiet and almost sleepy. She decided to drop her cards and dash home for a sandwich. Her mother would be wondering what had happened to her. She pushed open the door of the office.

Adam was seated at her desk, leaning back in her chair. Her heart began its customary thudding as she approached him.

'It's very late—' she began.

'Sit down, Leigh.' Now the hammering in her heart was caused by trepidation. She'd been right—his anger was due to something she had done, and she was sure she knew what

169

it was. She eased herself into Pauline's chair.

'I know why you want to see me, Adam,' she said quickly, believing attack was the best form of defence. If she could deny reading her mother's file, perhaps admit to taking it by mistake, but nothing more . . .

Adam frowned. 'That's impossible. Unless— Did you speak to Mrs Rochelle this morning?'

'Mrs Rochelle?' So it wasn't to do with her mother's file at all! But Mrs Rochelle? 'Has something happened to Mrs Rochelle?'

She recalled seeing the television presenter seated alone in the waiting area this morning, but had thought nothing of it. After all, she'd suggested she come to see Adam about Harry. What could the woman have said?

'You could put it that way, I suppose. You happened to Mrs Rochelle.'

'I? Please explain, Adam. I don't understand.'

'It's all to do with your making diagnoses without consulting me first. I'm her doctor. You're my health visitor, not my locum.'

'A partnership,' Leigh reminded him, trying to think where she had gone wrong with Mrs Rochelle. As far as she could recall, the woman had been extremely relieved at knowing Harry's problem did have a name, and she hadn't been imagining things.

That's if I was right, she thought with a sudden shock, and it is autism. Could it have

170

been something quite different? Even so, it was only a suggestion on my part—I told her that.

'Partnerships can only succeed when there's conference and discussion,' said Adam sharply. 'I think I should know when you plan to visit a family where there are problems.'

Leigh stared at him in amazement. Was she hearing things? She lifted her chin defiantly.

'Adam, nothing in my contract says I should tell you which families I propose to see each day. And, in this case, I was under the impression you were expecting me to visit. Daphne told you about the phone call from Mrs Rochelle, and you suggested I read a report in Harry Rochelle's file.'

'You're quite right, I did speak to Daphne. And it's obvious you didn't bother to read the file before you visited.'

'Well, no— But I read it afterwards, and what I read confirmed what I had thought. I also asked Mrs Rochelle to come and see you to find out more.'

'Oh, yes, she came. She came because she was desperately upset. You told her Harry is autistic.'

'I only suggested it. And, looking back, I feel reasonably confident that I was right to tell her—'

'You had no right to tell her!' His voice was cutting, and his eyes glittered.

'She begged me to! She was at her wits' end.

She was terrified that he might be mentally handicapped. But he doesn't appear mentally handicapped, and I said so. Are you trying to tell me that he is? That he isn't autistic at all?'

'I'm not saying that,' said Adam. 'I believe Harry Rochelle is autistic. In fact, I've already been planning to get him tested at the child psychology unit at the Queen Anne. Which you should have seen from the file.' He moved from the chair and perched himself on the edge of the desk, one long leg revealing pale blue socks and a short expanse of skin covered with golden hairs. Leigh found herself staring at it.

'Then what's the problem?' she asked.

'The problem is, you don't have the courage of your convictions. Your mistake was not telling her enough. You suggested autism, but you didn't tell her what it could mean—the education, the help, the prognosis. You left her in the dark.'

Leigh was silent. Because he was right. 'So what happened?' she finally asked quietly.

'Before she had the chance to see me or a paediatrician, a well-meaning friend came along, and at the mention of autism proceeded to tell her gruesome stories of children locked in institutions, of parents who couldn't cope and ended up in mental hospitals, of marriages breaking up because parents couldn't agree on the management of a child.'

Leigh was horrified. 'Adam, how could I

know that would happen? She was so relieved when I left. And, in my experience—'

'The point is, Leigh, you don't have enough experience. You're what—twenty-four? Twenty-five? What do you know of life?'

'I don't think that's the issue at all. If you're so sure it is autism, why didn't you suggest it yourself?'

'Because I'm not certain. I'm not an expert in the field. It's my job to refer conditions out of my realm to the people who know. Now do you see what I mean? The ultimate diagnosis comes from the experts.'

Without warning, a vision of her mother's file swam into Leigh's mind. She could see the words he had written. '?menopause. ?migraine. ?further investigations.' Suddenly his censure of her was too much to bear. A wave of anger flooded through her.

'The ultimate diagnosis?' she repeated, and knew she was going to say too much but knew she couldn't stop it. 'You talk about the ultimate diagnosis, about referring every patient who's out of your field to the experts. In that case, why wasn't my mother referred by you for the ultimate diagnosis? Or did you feel you were expert enough? What was your ultimate diagnosis? Migraine? Menopause? Or just hypochondria?'

She sat rigidly in her seat, breathing hard, waiting for his reaction. She shouldn't have said anything, she'd decided it wouldn't help matters, but it had been his fault, blaming her like that. She looked at him warily.

He looked as if he'd suffered a physical blow, but he quickly recovered himself. He scrutinised her for a moment, then nodded slowly. There was such a look of pain in his blue eyes that Leigh immediately regretted her angry words, and wished she could take it all back. She didn't move.

'Yes, I see now. It was you who had the notes. I was looking for them.'

'Why?' There was tension in the small room. Outside, a bird sang.

'I suddenly realised I'd seen your mother before. And it had to be ten years ago, when I was a locum here for six months.'

'Then you don't deny you sent her away without doing anything for her?'

'Is that what you think? That I was negligent?'

'I always felt someone was,' said Leigh. 'And then I saw it, written down in black and white. No further investigations were done.'

Adam nodded. 'I agree. None appears to have been done. And you believe that to be my fault?'

'Adam, I can't believe anything else! Oh, I tried to tell myself you must have had a reason for not doing more, but what reason could you have had? She nearly died—'

He stood up, and crossed the room to stand in front of her.

174

'Leigh, I can't tell you what to believe. But I have to tell you how deeply you've hurt me. I never imagined you could ever think me negligent. I thought you trusted me, but I must have been wrong. I must have misinterpreted your feelings for me.'

And he strode from the room.

CHAPTER TEN

Leigh watched the door swing to behind him. She heard his angry footsteps growing fainter. Out in the hall a child started to cry. Leigh felt numb, drained of all emotion. As Adam had marched from the room her only thought had been that he was walking away from her, walking out of her life.

She could see now what a fool she'd been to bring her mother into the argument. But she'd been so furious at his talk of 'ultimate diagnosis', his almost arrogant conviction that he had never made a mistake in his career. Brought to its logical conclusion, it had been an error on someone's part that had led to the delay in treatment for her mother. The notes in her mother's file could only point at Adam Christie. Yet he actively denied this. And he was blaming Leigh—for not trusting him!

Waves of emotion suddenly broke through. She put her head on the desk and wept.

Self-pity, anger, frustration, injustice—she couldn't have put a name to the reason for her misery. But she knew it was a blessed relief from the tension of the past few days, and she indulged herself.

The door opened, and she looked up sharply, her face wet with tears. For a brief instant she had hoped . . .

'Oh—I'm sorry, Leigh, I didn't realise anyone was in here.' Daphne sounded shocked and embarrassed.

'It's all right, I'm just going.' Leigh grabbed her bag and got up awkwardly from her chair.

'What's wrong, Leigh? Has something happened?'

'No—it's nothing! I'm just going for my lunch!' Daphne called something after her as she rushed from the room, but she didn't hear her.

In the corridor she stopped to blow her nose. She knew she must look a mess. The staff cloakroom was near by, so she slipped in to tidy herself and comb her hair. It was deserted. She looked at herself in the mirror. She did look rather bedraggled. She splashed cold water on her face and felt better, more in control.

She stood for a moment, gazing through the window that overlooked the front entrance and drive. A young woman was pushing a pram towards the clinic, a toddler perched on the foot of the pram, legs dangling, a slightly older child tagging along, grasping its mother's coat with a grubby hand. Leigh didn't know them, but her heart went out to them, because they looked so defeated.

The woman had stringy brown hair, and her eyes were shadowed. She paused halfway along the drive, and hesitated before turning towards the pram park. As she did so, Leigh heard the front door open and close, and seconds later Adam stepped out on to the drive. The woman saw him and stopped. A smile slowly spread across her pale features as he looked in their direction and began to walk towards them.

Leigh saw him reach them, saw him bend attentively to catch the woman's words, as she pulled back the pram covers. Adam peeped inside, and she smiled at something he said. He chucked the toddler under the chin and spoke to the eldest child, finally producing something from his coat pocket which the child took eagerly.

A few more words, serious this time, were exchanged between Adam and the woman, then he left her and walked back towards the car park. The woman seemed happier, the child was laughing. The woman pushed the pram towards the pram park, her step lighter, a smile on her thin face.

Leigh watched until they were all out of sight, only then aware that tears were near to the surface.

How could I have been so stupid? she told herself angrily, blinking away the tears. How could I ever have imagined him to be negligent?

That was Adam, she mouthed silently at her reflection in the mirror. Adam, as concerned off duty as on. Adam, who really cares for all his patients. And now I've spoiled it all. I should have accepted his criticism without bringing Mother's problem into it. I should have kept my big mouth shut.

She shoved her comb into her bag. Was it too late to try to make amends?

*   *   *

At first when she entered the house she thought it was empty. She threw her bag and jacket on a chair and went into the kitchen to make a drink. The remnants from a light meal were in the sink, so her mother had already had lunch. Not surprising; it was gone half-past one. She probably thought Leigh wasn't coming home for lunch.

There were cream crackers and a lump of cheese on a plate, so she nibbled at them while she waited for the kettle to boil. There were sounds of movement on the upstairs landing, and her mother's voice floated down.

'Is that you, Leigh? You're very late.' Evelyn came carefully into the kitchen, leaning on her stick. She was wearing an oatmeal tweed dress with a chunky brown necklace, and she was wearing make-up.

'I got held up,' said Leigh, and suddenly tears were very near to the surface—she couldn't think why.

'What are you making for yourself? There's ham in the fridge, tomatoes, more cheese.'

Leigh poured boiling water on her coffee. 'I'm not hungry. Gone past it, I suppose.' She glanced at her mother. 'You're looking very smart, Mother. Is it some special occasion I don't know about?'

Evelyn patted her hair self-consciously. 'Not really. Graham said he might call in to look at the garden. He's very keen on gardening.'

'Gardening? Mother, it's almost November!'

'Yes, I know. But he said he might have some good ideas for next spring. You have to plan ahead in a garden, you know.' Evelyn sat down and watched Leigh as she nibbled another cracker. 'I do wish you'd have a proper meal, Leigh.'

'I'm not hungry. Besides, I haven't much time—hearing tests at half-past two.'

'Time, time.' Evelyn frowned. 'What held you up? Are you all right? You look a bit washed out. Are they working you too hard?'

Leigh sank into a chair by the table, her mug of coffee in front of her, a cracker still in her fingers.

'No, the work's all right. I'm used to it. I had

179

a bit of a problem this morning, though, almost at lunch-time. That's why I'm late.'

Her mother said nothing, waiting for Leigh to expound further.

'An Indian family—four children, the mother suffering from an ectopic pregnancy. I had to ring the surgery, to get Adam—to come and see her—' She took a deep breath. 'We got her into hospital, and I arranged for a relative to look after the children, so it was quite late when I got back to the centre.'

She gulped at her coffee, fighting for control. Her mother watched her.

'Did something upset you?' Evelyn asked. 'You seem—on edge.'

'Not really—well, Adam felt I shouldn't diagnose his patients' illnesses. But I knew she was an ectopic—there was nothing else it could be—'

She looked at her mother, and sudden tears filled her eyes. She wiped them away angrily.

'What is it?' her mother asked gently. 'Come on, there's more to it than that, isn't there?'

Leigh nodded mutely. She drank some coffee.

'Is it Adam?'

'Things seemed to be going fine,' Leigh bunt out. 'I did worry a bit over what Mrs Christie said about Fenella coming back, but he did reassure me last night that he hadn't thought about her for years. So I

180

suppose I hoped—I did start to feel he might fall in love with me—' Her lips quivered.

'Does he know how you feel?'

Leigh shook her head. 'But I was such a stupid fool—and now I've lost him—'

She swallowed. 'Mother, you remember saying on Monday evening you thought I was worried about something, and I said it was because of what Mrs Christie had said?'

'You just said there was nothing to worry about on that score.'

'I know. It wasn't really that I was worried about. It was something else.'

'I can't imagine what it might be. Tell me,' said Evelyn.

'I discovered on Monday the name of the locum you saw ten years ago. You remember, the one who failed to get you looked at, and then it was too late, and you had your accident?'

'Yes, yes, Leigh, I know all this. I've told you, I don't remember him, or her. I wish I did.' Evelyn looked at Leigh. 'You know who it was?'

'I took out your file by mistake, and then I decided to read that part, and lay the ghost for good. I felt sure it would be someone we couldn't ever possibly trace—or ever want to—but I just wanted to know. And I wish I'd never done it. It was Adam Christie.'

They sat and looked at each other. Evelyn blinked a few times.

'Adam? Ten years ago? Then—then I *did* see him—I knew I had— Leigh, he said I hadn't.'

'No, Mother, he said he hadn't seen you at the Queen Anne. And it seems that started him wondering, and he finally realised from your notes when he did see you.'

'Did he tell you that?'

'Yes—in the middle of a blazing row! Mother, I've really blown it. When I first found out I thought the best thing would be for me to tell him what I'd read, get it out in the open. Then, after the rehearsal, he was so nice to me, so I thought I'd test the water by asking him about Fenella. And then—well, I thought if I told him about the file it might spoil what we had going for us. So I decided to forget about it all, forget I'd ever seen it.'

'That seems to be the wisest course,' Evelyn agreed. 'Telling him won't cure my leg, or bring my memory back.'

'Yes. But that's not all. This morning we had an argument over a family I'd visited, and I'm afraid I just blurted it all out, told him I believed he'd been negligent. I suppose I really wanted him to explain why he hadn't been negligent, but he didn't, just gave me a dreadful look. I could see I'd hurt him, accusing him like that, but it's too late now to put things right. It looks like the end for Adam and me.'

Evelyn looked at her for a moment. 'Yes, it

does look black, I agree. But surely if he does care for you a little he'll come to his senses and try to sort it out with you.'

'No,' said Leigh unhappily. 'I've done just what his mother asked me not to do—I've hurt him. I, of all people, have cast a slur on his professional competence. He'll never forgive me for that.'

She sighed and stood up. Time to go.

Evelyn frowned. 'Are you going to let one little argument ruin everything? You have a right to your opinions, as he has. And I don't see why a professional disagreement should affect your personal relationship.'

'It goes deeper than that, Mother. If he believes I can't trust him in his work, he'll think I can't trust him at all.'

'Why should he think that? Surely those two areas of his life are quite separate.'

Leigh shrugged. 'Oh, I don't know what to think. It doesn't matter now. All I wanted was his side of the story, but he seemed to think I was accusing him. Perhaps I put it all wrong. But his mother was right when she said he was too sensitive for his own good. So it looks as if it's the end. And I must go now, I've got a busy afternoon ahead.'

She rinsed her mug under the tap and placed it on the drainer.

'I reckon you're both as stubborn as each other,' said Evelyn. 'I expect you'll come to your senses.'

Leigh just smiled at her mother and left.

*   *   *

'Graham said he may call round tomorrow afternoon,' said Evelyn, as they cleared up after their evening meal.

'Graham? Oh, yes, about the gardening—I remember.'

'No, not the gardening, Leigh. He came this afternoon to look at the garden. He's got a lot of good ideas about shrubs—easy to care for. He seems very knowledgeable—a nice man.'

The way she said it made Leigh glance sharply at her, but she was replacing cutlery in a drawer, and Leigh couldn't see her expression.

'He's got a nice garden, has he?'

'Well, I haven't seen it, of course, but he tells me it's very small. He's always wanted a larger one, but they always seem to go with larger houses, and he doesn't want to take out a mortgage at his age.'

'How old is he?' asked Leigh.

'Sixty-two. He retired early.'

'You seem to get on very well with him.'

'Everyone gets on with him. He's very easygoing. Anyway—' Evelyn closed the drawer carefully '—I've invited him round for tea. He's coming at four, or thereabouts.'

'Do you want me out of the way?' Leigh wiped the draining board.

'You? Out of the way? Goodness, it's nothing like that!' But Leigh noticed her mother couldn't help flushing slightly.

'I was thinking of going into town, anyway,' said Leigh. 'It's Daphne's birthday next week, and I'd like to get her a little something. Perhaps some nice leather gloves. I noticed she wears a woolly pair sometimes, when it's chilly, and the palms are well darned.'

'She can't be poor,' said Evelyn. 'Perhaps she's a miser.' They giggled a bit at that and went in to watch television.

*   *   *

Leigh saw a lovely pair of navy leather gloves in a shop in Mossgate on Saturday morning, so she didn't go to town. It was another nice day, all golden and mellow, and she couldn't help being reminded of the other Sunday in Stow. And that made her think of Adam and what might have been.

After lunch she took writing paper and envelopes out to the little summer-house, to write some belated letters. It was a quarter to three. It would give Evelyn and Graham some time together when he arrived.

You're a matchmaker! she chided herself, as she made herself comfortable in a cane armchair. Your own love-life's gone astray, so you're pairing off your mother. What are you thinking of?

She smiled to herself and picked up her pen. 'Dear Mary,' she began, 'So sorry . . .'

Absorbed in her second letter, she was surprised when her mother appeared at the front door, looking perturbed.

'What's wrong?' asked Leigh. 'Is it Graham?'

'Oh, no, there's nothing wrong, not really. It's just—Adam's here.'

'Adam?' Hot colour rushed to Leigh's face. She put down her letter. 'Why?'

'He wants to see you, that's all. I think he wants to take you out. I told him the weather forecast said rain later.'

'Take me out?' She was aware that she sounded like a parrot. She got up. 'I'd better come.'

'No, why doesn't he come down here? It's very—private, and pleasant. Anyway, Graham's just come too, so I think—'

'Yes, all right. I'll wait here,' said Leigh.

Evelyn walked haltingly back to the house. Leigh watched her, acutely aware of her own racing pulse and burning cheeks. She wasn't prepared to see Adam now!

She tried to appear unconcerned as he strode down the steps and crossed the grass towards the summer-house. He was wearing navy cords and a kingfisher-blue sweater, and he walked with an easy, confident grace. Leigh could feel excitement swelling inside her. He wasn't smiling.

186

He stood in the open doorway and looked at her for a moment. His eyes seemed to be bluer than ever. Probably the sweater, she thought, making a valiant effort to ignore the quiverings of emotion inside her.

'Adam, what a surprise.' She tried to keep the tremble from her voice.

'May I come in?'

In reply, she drew forward another chair, and he folded his length into it. He was just inches away. Her mouth felt dry. She wondered why he'd come. Had he come to explain his behaviour yesterday? Or perhaps he had come for an apology. She knew she had hurt him, and she could even now feel the guilt staining her cheeks. But she didn't know how to start.

'Writing letters?' he asked.

'Yes. I'm afraid I've let them slide since I came back to Mossgate.'

He was silent for a moment, then he said, 'You have a lot of friends in Bath, I expect.'

'Yes, I suppose I have—but these letters aren't for those friends. They're for girls I trained with at the Queen Anne. And schoolfriends.'

'I seem to have lost touch with my schoolfriends. It's rather a long time ago.' Adam was watching her intently. 'You're a very loyal friend, aren't you?'

'Friends should be.' That sounded pompous, so she added, 'I try to be.'

'One of your friends from Bath rang the health centre on Thursday, and got put through to me by mistake,' he told her.

'Yes. I'm sorry about that. He lost my home number.'

'He sounded quite miffed because you weren't there. Couldn't seem to understand I was in the middle of a consultation. I'm afraid I offended him.'

'It doesn't matter. It wasn't important.'

Conversation seemed to pall. Leigh subdued a sudden urge to throw herself into his arms, to say none of it mattered, nothing mattered but them, she did trust him, she always had . . . He still wasn't smiling. Even his eyes were serious.

The sun vanished behind a dark cloud, and there was a sudden chill in the air. Leigh shivered, and Adam looked pensive.

'Adam, why have you come?' She had to ask.

'To see you.'

'Just to see me?'

'I feel I was rather rude to you yesterday. We both said things we didn't mean. I came to talk. We can't leave things the way they are.'

'You mean our professional relationship. I agree.'

'I mean our relationship, full stop.'

Suddenly, unaccountably, Leigh was afraid. She got up. 'It's gone chilly, Adam. I'm going to fetch a jacket.'

'I thought we might go for a drive

somewhere,' he said.

'Can't we talk here?'

'If you prefer it. Fetch your jacket—I think the sun has gone for good.'

The conversation seemed to have taken on the flavour of a dream, or a badly acted play. Their words were stilted and polite. They were like strangers. Leigh felt strangely embarrassed. Leaving him in the summer-house, she quickly crossed the lawn and went up the steps to the kitchen.

Evelyn and Graham were discussing music in the sitting-room. Leigh put her head round the door.

'We're not going out, Mother. We'll stay where we are. Hello, Graham.'

'Hello, Leigh. Yes, I think you're wise. It's coming on to rain.'

'I thought it might keep off,' said Evelyn optimistically.

'It's gone a bit chilly in there. I've come for a jacket,' Leigh explained.

'Shall I get Graham to bring you some tea?' asked Evelyn.

Leigh hesitated. Graham looked relaxed and comfortable. He seemed to have made himself at home. The surprising thing was, he seemed to fit in there. He made her think of her father.

'No, it's all right,' she said. 'We'll come inside in a little while.'

'I said everything would be all right again,

didn't I?' said Evelyn cheerfully.

'It isn't—yet. We've got a lot to talk about.'

Leigh hurried upstairs to her room and pulled a chunky gold sweater from a cupboard. It looked pretty good over her brown checked shirt and pleated skirt, gently following the curves of her slim body. She was aware of Adam's admiring glance as she returned to the summer-house and closed the door behind her. Her pulses had started to sprint again, so she took some deep breaths and sat carefully in her chair. She smiled at him.

'You look nice,' he said.

'Thank you.' So do you, she thought. I could look at you all day. His gaze met hers, and she had a terrifying thought that he could tell what she was thinking. She hadn't said it aloud, had she?

He leaned back in his chair and crossed his long legs.

'Haven't you stopped to wonder what came over us yesterday, Leigh?'

So he was willing to share the blame. She nodded. 'We were both very angry.'

'And we'd been getting on so well. Don't you agree, we'd been getting on very well?'

Leigh wasn't sure whether he meant personally or professionally, so she didn't reply.

'Of course, I can see now why you felt as you did,' he went on. 'And that's why I've come. But you were mistaken, even though it does look as though I was to blame.'

Leigh sat rigidly in her chair. 'Oh.'

'It's obvious you've read your mother's medical file. I suppose it was inevitable that you would, after what you told me the other day, about the locum. And I can see what you must have thought from my notes. But, believe me, Leigh, there was nothing more I could have done.'

Leigh let out her breath. 'You could have referred her to someone.'

'Will you believe me if I tell you I did?'

'Who? There's no one mentioned in the notes.'

'A neurosurgeon at the Queen Anne—Jephcott.'

'It was Mr Jephcott who operated when she had her accident. And don't forget I read her hospital notes—by accident.' Was that a fleeting smile on his mouth? 'There was nothing in her hospital notes about her seeing anyone there before she was rushed into Casualty. It was remarked upon, if you remember.'

'I do remember, Leigh. And that's what I don't understand. I know I referred her—you must have seen the R in a circle in my notes?' Leigh nodded. 'Now do you understand why I was so angry? You were accusing me of being negligent in my job, and I knew I'd done everything possible for her. Of course, later, when I looked at those notes again, I could see why you'd come to that conclusion.'

'It was logical,' said Leigh in a small voice, hoping this could be the end of the matter.

'Very logical. And when I first realised I'd been the locum you'd mentioned I figured the safest way would be not to say anything— unless you did.'

'I felt the same!' Leigh burst out. 'I didn't want to mention it again—it was driving a wedge between us. I wanted to trust you, I wanted to forget all I'd seen in that file. Adam, you can't imagine how I felt when I saw your name. I wanted it to be anyone but you!'

He uncrossed his legs and leaned towards her. 'I suppose, in a way, we ought to be thankful for the Rochelles' dilemma. If she hadn't come, and given me a reason to be mad with you, then you wouldn't have said anything, and I wouldn't have known what you felt.' He paused, and softly rested his hand on hers. 'And it would always have been there between us—the doubt, the uncertainty, the waiting for one of us to mention it. I think it's better out in the open, don't you?'

Leigh could almost feel his breath on her cheek. He smelled of something musky and tangy, masculine and sensuous. She felt a stirring inside her.

'Oh, yes!' she breathed. 'I'm glad you came. I felt so awful, the way I hurt you—'

'My pride,' he murmured, stroking her hand. 'You hurt my pride.'

192

'And I thought we could never be friends again—'

'Friends? Is that all we are? Friends?' There was a throbbing in his voice. Leigh could hardly breathe.

'Do you want more than friendship?'

'Don't you?' His voice made her quiver and tingle. 'Come here.'

The cane sofa had never been meant for anything more than reading or resting. It didn't look very strong. But Leigh didn't hesitate. She sat beside him and he gently drew her towards him, his sensual lips first touching and teasing her lips and her ears, her neck and her eyes, until her whole body was screaming silently for him to take her, crush her in his arms, satisfy her desperate longing for him.

Her skin tingled, her breasts ached and throbbed, strange, exciting sensations seemed to ripple through her body. And then his lips came down on hers, his tongue searching and tasting, his sensitive hands stroking and caressing. She couldn't prevent the little moan that escaped her.

The pressure of his mouth grew more demanding, his eager hand skilfully slipped beneath her shirt to fondle her erect nipple. The desire inside her grew to a tremendous crescendo until she felt like shouting her ecstasy to the world.

Adam must have sensed the intensity of her

feelings. Gently he released her, and she lay against him, still excited, still wanting him.

'I'm sorry,' he murmured. 'I didn't mean that to happen.'

Leigh didn't answer. She moved slightly away from him, straightening her hair and her clothing. Her heart still raced.

'That was a strange way of talking,' she remarked, her voice shaky.

'Oh, no, that's the best way to talk.' There was a quirk in his smile, but his blue eyes were still dark and intense.

'Then, if the talking's over, we'll go and have some tea. Now we know the blame is not on you, but some faceless person at the hospital who forgot to send her an appointment—'

Adam sat up. 'Did I say that? I think it's highly unlikely. You see, I wrote the letter there and then, and gave it to her myself, for her to ring up and make an appointment that suited her. And she said she would. It was the way we did it then. She took it with her, the letter for Mr Jephcott.'

CHAPTER ELEVEN

Leigh stared at him. 'Well, it's pretty obvious, isn't it? She must have lost it. But it's strange she didn't ask you for another one. Perhaps she started to feel better.'

She knew that was unlikely, but it wasn't Adam's fault, she could see that now. She believed him, she'd seen the R in a circle. She didn't need to know any more.

'I wasn't there, Leigh,' Adam told her. 'I left the practice a couple of weeks later. To be honest, I never gave it another thought—I was very busy in Salford.'

'Yes, let's forget it, shall we? Nothing can be done. Let's go and have tea before the rain starts.'

Hand in hand they walked back across the grass to the house. The sky was dark and heavy.

*　　　*　　　*

'Everything seems to be working out just right,' said Evelyn happily on Monday morning, as she spread butter on her toast. Leigh had just come in with the morning's post.

'What do you mean by everything?' Leigh sorted the letters. A gas bill, a bank statement, and a letter for her mother. A thin letter for herself, postmarked Bath, the envelope typewritten. She couldn't think who it might be.

'Well, you and Adam—and I'm so much happier these days—' Evelyn didn't mention Graham, but Leigh knew what she meant. And

195

she was glad her mother had found another friend. She'd shut herself away for far too long.

I'm glad I came back home, Leigh said to herself, as she opened her own letter. My mother's found Graham, and I've found Adam. A little thrill ran through her when she recalled last Saturday evening. Adam had stayed for tea, they had all talked for ages, then Adam had taken her out for a meal in a small, intimate restaurant on the road to Stratford-on-Avon, and they'd talked some more and discovered little things about each other. They'd laughed as they'd tried to avoid the rain, running back to the car, and Leigh had never felt so happy before. Then they'd driven back home leisurely, able to relax now all the misunderstandings had been eradicated.

They'd talked about holidays, and places they'd seen, and books they'd read. They'd kissed, and kissed again, and Leigh had found herself hungering for Adam's kisses and his touch. He was becoming an addiction!

She smiled to herself. Her mother had been right to be optimistic. Yet when she thought of Friday— No, she wouldn't think of Friday. It was all over and done with, everything was clear, and she could see their future ahead, all shiny and bright with promise. And she couldn't stop the ecstatic shiver that ran through her.

'Oh,' said her mother, laying down the

opened envelope.

'Is something wrong?' asked Leigh, opening her own letter.

'It's from Kate. They think they've found a house.'

'Already?'

'It's got four bedrooms, and a sun-lounge, and a huge garden, and—oh, lots of things. But it's more expensive than they expected, although she says with my contribution they could possibly manage it.'

'You want to go?' asked Leigh.

'I don't know. What will you do, Leigh? I'd have to sell this one—' Evelyn glanced around the cosy kitchen. 'I'm sort of fond of this one; it's full of happy memories. But Kate's very keen for me to go—'

'Don't worry about me, Mother,' said Leigh, patting her hand. 'If you want to go, you go. I can easily find a little flat or something for the next few months. Anyway, you know what it's like trying to sell a house these days. It can take months!'

She forced a laugh. She didn't want her mother to sell the old house. It did have happy memories, and she liked the idea of always having it here to come back to. But things have to change, and I have to grow up, she added silently. And, of course, there would always be Adam. Would Adam want to buy this house for them to live in? No, she was thinking too far ahead. She knew he had a nice comfortable flat just over the Worcestershire border in Froggley. Perhaps he wouldn't want to buy a house straight away, and, anyway, not in Mossgate.

'No,' said her mother. 'I don't want to go to Oxford. Not now I've made new friends at the Tuesday club, and Graham—' She fiddled with her toast.

'Are you sure, Mother? Could you cope with this house on your own?'

'I always used to. And I feel much more confident now. And I'm sure, if I had problems, Graham would help. Perhaps we could get someone in, just a morning a week perhaps. Yes, Leigh, I'm sure I could manage. I was never very happy about going to Oxford. It was always Kate's idea.'

'Then you'll have to write to her and tell her what you've decided. Perhaps they could find a smaller house they can afford.'

Leigh couldn't help feeling a little relieved. She pulled her own letter from its envelope and unfolded it. It was from Colin.

'Oh, you've got a letter,' remarked Evelyn, opening the gas bill. 'From someone in Bath?'

'Yes. A friend in Bath.' Leigh read it quickly. Colin was considering applying for a post in Birmingham. That way, Leigh could stay in Mossgate, and they could see each other more often. But he wanted her opinion on the idea. When he'd rung the health centre, and been insulted by that uppity doctor, he'd wondered if there'd been anything going on between him and Leigh, to make him so offensive. He wanted Leigh to reassure him on that point, before he applied.

Leigh pushed the letter in the pocket of her skirt. She couldn't help feeling a bit guilty over her offhand treatment of Colin. But she'd never really encouraged him to think she was serious about him. She'd given him her home number again, but he hadn't rung. She hadn't— She paused. No, she hadn't given him her home address again, so how had he managed to send this letter? Perhaps he hadn't mislaid it at all. Or the phone number.

She tipped bran flakes into her dish and added milk. It was rather unsettling, Colin acting deviously like that. She'd always trusted him. Were all men a little devious? She remembered Adam's touch, his kisses, the way he looked at her. She would trust him with her life. She had given him her life. She loved him.

She would have to write to Colin, be tactful, point out she wasn't staying in Mossgate anyway, and if he waited she would soon be back in Bath. She could see Miss Wainwright's lined face, hear her words: 'I have a strong hunch you won't be coming back.'

It was true, the thought of living and working in Bath while Adam was miles away, here in Mossgate, didn't bear thinking about.

Evelyn pushed her toast away and poured herself another cup of tea. 'Seems very warm in here,' she remarked. 'I feel quite thirsty this morning.'

Leigh looked at her and smiled, her mind on the letter from Colin, and anticipating seeing Adam again at the centre. Her heart gave a little skip. She finished her breakfast and put the dishes in the sink. She didn't have to wash them now, and Evelyn was managing things so well these days, so Leigh didn't give it another thought. She ran up to brush her teeth and get ready for work.

Adam was in the reception office when she arrived, discussing something earnestly with Janet, the senior receptionist. He came out and saw Leigh as she passed on her way to the health visitors' office.

'Good morning, Leigh.'

'Good morning, Adam.' Their eyes met for a long moment. Their fingers touched briefly, and an electric current seemed to run through Leigh's body.

'Any problems with your families that you want to talk about?' His tone was professional, but his eyes weren't.

'None that I can think of at the moment,' said Leigh.

'I shall be here until eleven o'clock if you want me.'

If I want you! She could only hope her eyes gave him the answer. She gave him a tremulous smile and went along to her office. She felt his eyes watching her go. She sat at her desk, willing her heart to behave. She'd never been in love before, never knew it felt like this! She'd thought she'd been in love, two or three times. And she'd heard her friends sighing and fretting over their love-affairs, and had privately thought they'd been laying it on a bit thick! Being in love couldn't make one feel like that!

Now she knew. But she had no intention of sighing and fretting to anyone. Her feelings would be strictly private—although her actions might give her away!

Daphne came in, grumbling about the rain, and Pauline followed, still worrying that her father's dog might be pining for him.

'You look happy,' Pauline remarked to Leigh. 'Won the pools?'

*   *   *

Adam came into the office at eleven o'clock, on the pretext of wanting to talk about Harry Rochelle. He somehow wangled it that Leigh had to go to his consulting-room to see a report, and once there he closed the door and kissed her firmly and passionately until she felt she was melting.

'You shouldn't do that,' she protested weakly, not meaning it. 'Anyone could come in.'

'I did it because I'm going to be very busy at the hospital this evening, and I'm on call tomorrow and Wednesday. So I shan't have much chance of seeing you, except here.'

He drew her to him again, kissing her softly. Leigh sighed.

'I do love you, Adam,' she whispered. There, she'd said it. In response, his kiss became more fervent, his grasp stronger. Then he held her away from him and looked into her shining eyes.

'If you look like that, everyone's going to know,' he said huskily. And he kissed her again. Leigh could feel her knees trembling. Finally he let her go and she went back to the office to finish her clerical work. Pauline looked up as she entered.

'Got a problem? You look a bit bothered.'

'No—no, I'm fine.' She sat down. It's called love, she wanted to say.

*   *   *

Next day, Leigh took her mother along to the Tuesday club. Evelyn seemed more ungainly than usual, finding great difficulty in climbing from the car. However, she perked up a little once they were inside, and she quickly buttonholed Graham, asking him if the tea was made yet as she was thirsty. Leigh gave her a curious glance, but she was concerned with her own work, and knew her mother would soon start enjoying herself.

For once, she was back at the centre quite

202

early, and went along to the room where the Tuesday club was held. She was surprised to find they had finished. Edna was piling up chairs, and only a few of the members were still there, chatting and putting on coats, waiting for the transport to take them home. There was no sign of Graham or Evelyn.

'You've finished early,' said Leigh to Edna. Edna pushed a pile of chairs against the wall.

'Didn't have many today—there's a virus about, didn't you know? A sort of chesty flu. It looked as if your mother's going down with it. She was quite flushed. Didn't you notice?'

Guiltily, Leigh recalled her mother's loss of appetite and unusual thirst. She should have realised. But she'd been rather wrapped up in her own feelings, and it hadn't registered.

'Who took her home?' she asked.

'Graham, of course. Quite sweet on her, isn't he? Oh, he was concerned, you could tell. I can hear wedding bells in that direction, I can tell you.'

'Edna, I'm sure it's nothing like that—'

'Well, of course, unless you've been in love yourself you might not see it in others. Me, I can see it. You wait and see if I'm not right.'

Her mother and Graham. In love. Well, why not? And the signs had been there, the last few days. Hadn't she accused herself of matchmaking only the other day?

She went to her office, sorted out her cards, and left.

As she stepped into the house, Graham came out into the hall. He was smiling, and Leigh was relieved that he didn't look too worried.

'Is my mother ill?' she asked him. 'Why didn't she say something this morning?'

'Your mother's not one to complain,' said Graham, as if he'd known her for years.

No, thought Leigh, she never used to complain. Ten years ago, we didn't know how she was suffering. Only Adam knew.

She went into the sitting-room. Evelyn was resting on the sofa with her feet up, a rug over her legs.

'What's wrong, Mother? Shall I get Adam to come and see you? He's on call tonight.'

'There's no need for all that. A bit of a cold, that's all I've got.'

Leigh rested her hand on her mother's forehead. 'You've got a temperature, Mother. You need a doctor.'

'Leigh, I don't want a doctor. It's just a cold. I've had colds before. I've been sneezing, and my throat's a bit sore, that's all. Certainly not enough to warrant calling out a doctor, believe me.'

Leigh and Graham exchanged glances. Graham shrugged. 'Is she always as stubborn as this?' he asked, smiling indulgently at Evelyn.

' 'Fraid so. Well, we'll wait and see if it's really a cold. If you're no better in the

204

morning, Mother, I shall tell Adam, and there'll be no argument about it,' Leigh said.

'I shall be fine tomorrow,' Evelyn insisted. 'But I shan't have any chicken pie tonight, just some soup, Leigh. And perhaps some ice-cream. And Graham will stay this evening, of course, and then we can listen to some Tchaikovsky and Mozart.'

Leigh frowned, observing the brightness in her eyes. She doubted she'd be better tomorrow.

*　　*　　*

And, of course, she wasn't. And she now had a very nasty cough which had woken her during the night. Leigh had given her hot lemon and honey, but it was obvious she needed more than that.

'I shall tell Adam as soon as I get in, Mother,' she promised, although her mother protested.

'Ring Graham,' she said huskily. 'Ask him to fetch me a bottle of cough syrup—that's all I need. Graham will come and stay while you're at work. He's a godsend.'

He certainly is, thought Leigh, as she drove to work. It was plain to see her mother did have the virus that was doing the rounds, and probably a bacterial infection superimposed. She was going to need antibiotics.

Adam had already started his surgery by the

time Leigh arrived at the centre, but she persuaded Janet to let her slip in to see him between patients.

'I shall only be a moment,' she assured her. 'I want him to come and see my mother. And I have a pile of visits to do.'

'Slip in after number 17, then,' said Janet, glancing at the board. 'Number 18's Mrs Pusey, and she'll take ages!'

The waiting hall was crowded, and everyone seemed to be sneezing or coughing. I hope I don't catch it, thought Leigh, watching for number 17 to come out. The light came on by Adam's name, and she slipped in quickly.

His face lit up with happy surprise when he saw who had entered. He had already picked up the next medical file, and when Leigh came and stood by him he said jokingly, 'Well, Mrs Pusey, what can I do for you this time?'

Leigh gave a nervous giggle, as the image of her consulting Adam, and letting him examine her, caused a violent flush to spread up her body.

'Please, Doctor, it's my heart,' she murmured. 'It keeps doing strange things.'

'How very odd! So does mine! Do you think it's catching?'

'I don't know about hearts, Adam, but this flu is certainly catching.'

He became serious again. 'Flu? This virus, you mean.'

'My mother's got it,' Leigh told him. 'She

wasn't well yesterday, but wouldn't admit it. And now she's got a temperature and she's very chesty—been coughing all night. Could you call in some time to look at her? Graham's staying at the house—Graham Scott.'

He took her hand and absent-mindedly kissed her fingers. 'Graham—ah, yes. They're very good friends, aren't they?'

'They seem to be. He's—he's a lot like my father.'

He nodded and stood up, looking down at her. 'Yes, I'll certainly put her on my list. Now, perhaps we'd better see what can be done about our mutual heart condition. I think this is the best treatment.'

He drew her into his arms, kissing her nose and her eyes, and finally her lips. 'Perhaps this isn't the best treatment after all,' he murmured. 'It seems to make my heart race even faster. What about yours?'

'Likewise. It must be the side-effects.'

'My advice,' he said softly, gently tracing her mouth with his finger, 'would be to make mad, passionate love to you, right here and now—'

'Yes, please!' whispered Leigh, lifting her face to his.

'But Mrs Pusey will be very, very angry if I keep her waiting too long!'

He released her suddenly. Leigh stood for a moment, trying to control herself.

'Can we continue the treatment at a later date?' she suggested. 'I have a feeling one dose isn't going to be enough.'

'What about tomorrow night?'

'Sounds all right to me. I might just last until then.' Blowing him a kiss, she hurried from the room, aware of curious glances from some of the waiting patients.

I don't care! she told herself blithely. I don't care if they know. I don't care if everyone knows!

*　　*　　*

Leigh wanted to get her visits finished early, so that she could squeeze in some extra time with her mother. Evelyn had become quite grumpy and cantankerous since she'd picked up the virus, and Leigh was finding it difficult to keep her patience.

She's ill, she kept telling herself. I must think of her as a hospital patient, and treat her likewise. She decided to call in at the delicatessen and pick up some little fancies to tempt her to eat.

But then she got involved with a young single mother who was having boyfriend trouble, and seemed to want to talk. She felt it was rather ironic that she should be asked to sort out others' relationship problems, when her own had so recently been such a mess. But she listened sympathetically. She wasn't at all happy about the unexplained bruises on the child's arms. The girl was already known to

Social Services, but was reluctant to contact them again.

I shall have to do it, thought Leigh, as she drove back to the centre. That child is at risk, and she's my main priority. The boyfriend had sounded like an unsavoury character, and, to complicate matters, he wasn't the child's father.

I hope I'm not making a fuss about nothing, she wondered, as she waited at the traffic lights.

So she rang Social Services as soon as she got back, but the person she wanted wasn't available. They spent precious minutes looking for someone else, while Leigh waited on the phone, and were unsuccessful. In the end she had to leave a message, which wasn't very satisfactory as the girl, although very willing to help, didn't seem very bright, and kept getting names and addresses mixed up before she finally got it right.

Cross and frustrated, Leigh didn't get home any earlier. Graham was still there, and she was appreciative. He had tempted her mother's appetite with a little salmon and cottage cheese, and slices of melon.

'I'm afraid I can't stay this afternoon,' he said apologetically as he followed Leigh into the sitting-room. 'It's my bridge class. I had hoped Evelyn might have come with me. Perhaps next week, if she's well enough.'

'I've told you, I'm not ill,' Evelyn protested.

'I think you should be in bed,' said Leigh.

'If I go to bed I shall begin to believe I'm ill. And up there, with no one to keep me company, and no view of the street and what's going on, I shall be bored to tears. No, I'm happier here—I'm not really ill, even though Dr Christie insisted I was.'

Dr Christie? thought Leigh. She always calls him Adam.

'What did he say was wrong with you?' she asked.

'Bronchitis. He's put me on penicillin. Graham fetched it from the chemist.'

Graham moved towards the door. 'I really have to go—'

'I'll see you out,' said Leigh, going into the hall with him. He took his coat from a hook.

'I'm afraid your mother was a little rude to Dr Christie,' said Graham rather uneasily. 'I suppose it's because she's not well.'

'Rude? What did she say to him?'

'I didn't understand a lot of it, but it was about finding out who he really was, and what he'd done to her ten years ago—Leigh, perhaps you'd better ask her about it. Dr Christie seemed very upset. He left very quickly.'

Leigh had listened with dawning horror. How could her mother have spoiled things again?

'I thought I ought to tell you, since you have to work with Dr Christie,' said Graham, opening the front door. 'But I put it down to her illness.'

'Don't worry about it, Graham. You were an angel to come. And I'm sure it was nothing important.' She closed the door behind him and went back to the sitting-room. Evelyn lay with her eyes closed, her cheeks slightly flushed. She's ill, Leigh reminded herself. I have to be careful how I go about this. She sat in an armchair.

'What time did Adam come?' she asked casually. Evelyn opened her eyes.

'Oh—about half-past eleven. He didn't stay long.'

'He probably didn't need to. He's an excellent doctor; it wouldn't take him long to find out what's wrong with you.'

'I asked him if he was sure this time,' said Evelyn, giving Leigh a sidelong glance.

'You what?'

'Well, he didn't know ten years ago, did he? You told me he thought it was migraine. A brain tumour—migraine!'

Leigh swallowed hard. 'Mother, that's all over and done with. Adam wasn't negligent—oh, why did you have to rake it all up again?'

'I just thought he ought to know that I knew who he was. He remembered me—you said so. I told him I remembered him.'

'Mother, you didn't remember him! You don't remember him!'

'Well, no, but that doesn't matter.' Evelyn

struggled to a sitting position. 'Leigh, what's all this about a letter?'

'A letter? What letter?'

'Dr Christie said I ought to talk to you about a letter. He said you should have told me about it. He'd given me one, he said, ten years ago. Well, of course, he didn't. You said yourself there was no record in the file of any referral at all. I told him he had to be making it up to excuse his lack of care.'

'Mother, I hope you realise what you've done. Now I have to go and see Adam, and apologise for all the things you've said. I realise you wouldn't have said them if you hadn't been ill—'

'I'm not ill. I just thought it better there were no secrets between us all. It's always best to clear the air. Oh, and I'd better tell you, when he mentioned the letter, I thought he meant that letter you had on Monday morning, from Bath. When you wouldn't talk about it, I guessed it had to be from Colin. I thought you must have told Dr Christie about it, so it must have said something important.'

'Mother, what are you talking about?'

'I told him I was very surprised if you were still serious about Colin, I had the impression it was all over and done with, but if he was still writing to you perhaps he was still serious about you. I'm sorry, Leigh; I assumed you'd told Dr Christie about Colin.'

'There was nothing to tell! Yes, Colin did

212

write—oh, Mother, what am I going to say to him this time? Everything was fine!'

'You shouldn't upset me like this, Leigh. You know I'm ill. I did what I thought was right. Yes, go and see Dr Christie, tell him your mother's off her rocker, but it's not surprising after all that's happened to her. I'm sure he'll know what you mean.' She closed her eyes and curled up again on the sofa.

Leigh watched her for a moment, trying to quell the vexation she felt at her mother's words. No, I should feel sorry for her, she told herself. She's ill, and doesn't realise what she's saying. She'll have forgotten it all when she's well.

She went into the kitchen to find something to eat. She wasn't hungry.

*   *   *

Evelyn was asleep when Leigh left the house to return to the centre. She was still feeling very disturbed, and apprehensive about Adam's reaction when she tried to explain. Although there wasn't really anything to explain. He knew she had accepted his own explanation about the referral letter. It was the mention of Colin that could complicate matters. She could only hope he had realised her mother had been uninhibited and talkative because of her fever.

He wasn't around when she arrived, and it

was only as she crossed the hall in the middle of the baby clinic that she caught sight of him going towards his consulting-room. Her stomach began to churn. She called out to him and he stopped, looking towards her. A smile began and then faded. She walked up to him.

'Adam, I'd like to thank—'

'We can't talk here.' He spoke curtly. She followed him into his surgery. He hung his coat on a peg.

'Adam, I'm sorry if my mother—'

He turned suddenly to face her. 'Leigh, can we get something straight? Why is it that whenever your mother comes into the conversation I'm attacked on all sides by accusations of negligence and malpractice? I was under the impression you'd accepted my explanation—of *your* misunderstanding. This morning your mother attacks me yet again about the letter she was given, and even seems to compare me unfavourably with someone called Colin, who I believe was your heart-throb in Bath, and who's still sending you passionate letters, urging you to return soon. I—'

'Adam, it wasn't like that at all! Let me explain!'

'I suppose he was the amorous swain who rang here the other day and was most annoyed with my presence? Leigh, after all the time we've spent together, I had hoped there was trust between us. That obviously isn't the case.

And, much as I'm attracted to you, if we have no trust we have nothing. No trust, no meaningful relationship. Do I make myself clear?'

She stared mutely at him. Was he saying it was all over between them? It sounded like that. Trying to hold back the tears, she rushed from the room.

No trust, no relationship. Just because she hadn't told him about Colin? Yes, of course, he'd told her about Fenella. Perhaps that was what he meant. But Colin had never meant anything to her! Oh, Mother, what have you done? she thought.

No trust, nothing. He was right. Leigh pushed open the cloakroom door, bolted herself in a cubicle, and banged her fists against the wall with frustration.

CHAPTER TWELVE

It wasn't easy, trying to appear confident and cheerful, when she felt so miserable inside. Leigh found herself recalling her own description of her turbulent feelings not so long ago. A rollercoaster. Was love always like a rollercoaster, with its highs as well as its lows? The highs were great, but, in her case, never lasted long enough for her to enjoy them. Just as she was getting used to them, down she went again, down to the very bottom.

I don't like it here at the bottom, she confessed to herself. Perhaps it's my own fault; I'm hoping for too much all the time, and she turned to smile at Mrs Read's fat baby. Such a lot of overweight babies just lately, she thought. Some dietary advice needed. But it was quite a nice baby really, especially when it smiled. It had no teeth yet, and the mother was worried.

'Babies don't stick to textbooks,' Leigh reassured her. 'She seems normal otherwise. But she is a little bit overweight, you know.'

She left the centre as soon as it was decently possible, explaining to Pauline that she'd left her mother alone, and she wasn't well. Pauline urged her to go, insisting that she knew just how Leigh felt, she'd been just as worried over her father's dog.

The grey weather seemed to match Leigh's mood. Gone was the golden autumn of Stow last Sunday. November next week, and it felt like it.

She didn't expect to see Graham's car in the drive when she got home. He must have returned as soon as his bridge class was over. She let herself into the house and hung up her jacket. They were talking in the sitting-room. Her mother laughed at something. She had to be feeling better, thought Leigh. Graham was obviously good for her.

Adam was good for me, she thought

216

wistfully. He brought a sparkle into my life, a glimpse of a future full of optimism and laughter. She didn't understand why her mother could have risked it all by raking up all the old doubts again, putting ideas into Adam's head, ideas about Colin. Could Colin have been the real reason for Adam's anger with her? Her mother must have assumed what was in that letter, got it all wrong, and made Adam believe she and Colin had had something going for them back in Bath. What on earth had made her do it? She knew how Leigh felt about Adam. Perhaps when Adam had mentioned the referral letter to the hospital, which she had denied ever receiving, perhaps being blamed for that had made her want to get back at him somehow.

Oh, I'm just hypothesising, thought Leigh, as she pushed open the sitting-room door. Evelyn still rested on the sofa; Graham had drawn up an easy chair, and between them, on a small table, lay scattered photographs.

'That was Torquay,' Evelyn was saying, as Leigh entered. She turned. 'Oh, it's you, Leigh!'

Leigh fixed a smile on her face. 'Feeling better, Mother?'

'I am, but you look like a wet dishcloth.'

'Thank you very much. But I'd rather not receive compliments like that.' Leigh tried to speak lightly.

Graham stood up. 'There's tea in the pot,

Leigh, if you'd like one.'

'I'd love one. I'll get it—you carry on enjoying yourself, looking at the photographs.'

'I thought it might take Evelyn out of herself,' said Graham diffidently. Leigh smiled at him. He was a nice, kind man. It wasn't his fault her mother wasn't herself lately.

She went into the kitchen and poured herself some tea, then stood by the window for a while, drinking it, looking out at the fresh, wet garden. She could see the summer-house, where Adam had kissed her. They had walked across the lawn, hand in hand, in love. Well, I was in love, she corrected herself. Was Adam? He'd never said so. And I'm still in love with him. I think I shall always be.

She wiped away an angry tear, and rinsed her cup under the tap. Why did life have to be so complicated? Why couldn't it be simple— boy meets girl, boy and girl fall in love, everyone lives happy ever after? Like the storybooks. No, come to think of it, even stories had their complications.

She rejoined the others in the sitting-room. Evelyn was going all misty-eyed over some that had been taken when she was very young, before the girls had been born.

'Tom was very good-looking, don't you agree, Graham?' she was asking.

'And so were you. And still are,' said Graham gallantly.

'You're just saying that. Of course, we were

very young there. Young, and so much in love. Tom became quite jealous sometimes—before we were married, of course—if I showed an interest in another man. It does them good to feel jealous, you know. They appreciate you more. And you know they really are in love with you.' She cast a quick glance at Leigh.

Jealous. Could Adam be jealous of Colin? Could that be why—? Leigh turned to her mother.

'Is that why you told Adam all about Colin? To make him jealous?'

'Naturally. I was just testing him. And was he? Jealous?'

'I don't know. He was just plain angry. I tried to explain, but he wouldn't listen.'

'Then he must be jealous. That means he loves you.' Evelyn spoke simply and happily.

'I'm not sure I understand that logic,' said Leigh. 'It doesn't follow.'

'Wait and see,' said her mother. 'Method in my madness. Oh, I say, just look at this one, Graham. What an awful frock!'

Leigh reached across to take one of the snapshots. She looked at it without seeing it. Could her mother be right? Adam was jealous because he loved her? Then why hadn't he shown it? He had seemed angry about her mother's disbelief in the existence of the referral letter, but perhaps that had been just an excuse . . .

'Was this taken at Eastbourne, Mother?' she

219

asked. Her mother glanced at it.

'Looks like Bournemouth to me. Hey, where are the Eastbourne pictures, Leigh? They don't seem to be here. And there's that lovely one of Tom and me on the front—well, it's a good one of Tom, anyway. I'm wearing that awful mauve frock with the big collar, you remember?'

'Aren't they in the sideboard?' suggested Leigh.

'No, that's where these were. And there was that picture of the four of us, just before Kate got married. You remember, we asked that nice young man to take it, the one with the blond hair, looked a bit like Adam when he was younger.' She stopped, frowned. 'Do I remember Adam when he was younger?'

Leigh watched her expression. 'I don't know. Do you?'

Evelyn shrugged. 'For a minute I thought I did. Never mind. Oh, I do wish I could find that one of your father—it was the year he bought me that navy leather handbag, you know, the one I never liked. I shoved it away in the wardrobe upstairs.' She looked excitedly at Leigh. 'You don't think—could they be in the handbag?'

'I'll go and look for you, if you like.'

Leigh went heavily upstairs into the spare bedroom. Her mother had stored lots of unwanted objects and clothes in the old oak wardrobe. Leigh rummaged under some blankets, finally pulling out the ugly navy handbag with its bows and gilt buckles.

She opened it and tipped the contents on the spare bed. Old diaries, a pair of blunt scissors, some old letters, a packet of photographs, a man's handkerchief, a pencil. She put the photographs aside and started to push the rest back. The letters were mostly from her mother's brother, who had emigrated to Canada fifteen years ago. She had kept the earlier ones. One of them, not an airmail one, didn't even have a postmark. Or a stamp. It had been written but not posted. Leigh looked at it with curiosity—and gasped.

It was crumpled, still sealed, and addressed to Mr Jephcott, Neurosurgeon, Queen Anne Hospital, Birmingham.

Leigh sank on to the bed and stared at it. This was it—Adam's letter. She had been right to believe him. No wonder he had been insulted by her mother's doubt in his integrity. She would go and show her mother now.

At the top of the stairs she paused, as she heard her mother laugh at one of the photographs. No. What good would it do? It would just make her feel guilty. She pushed it in her pocket and went slowly downstairs.

'You found them? Oh, goody!' Evelyn barely glanced at Leigh's troubled expression, but took the envelope and pulled out the prints.

'I'll go and put something on for dinner,'

said Leigh.

*   *   *

Daphne was overwhelmed by the gloves and the birthday card. She went pink.

'Oh, navy gloves—leather. How wonderful! How very kind of you, Leigh.'

'I hope they fit,' murmured Leigh, sitting at her desk. She had hoped to see Adam when she arrived, but Janet had told her quite frostily that Dr Christie had changed his surgery hours today, in order to put in an extra session at the hospital. He would be around this afternoon if she needed to see him. She emphasised the 'needed' as if Leigh were in the habit of running to him every five minutes.

I shall be visiting, thought Leigh. Why is it that every time I really do need to see him he's not around? Fate?

She hadn't slept well, had lain awake wondering how she could approach him. She had to tell him all about Colin, that was certain. But the letter—did she have to show him? Wouldn't that make him think she'd doubted his word before, and only now, with the letter found, she believed him? Oh, it was like the snail on the wall—one inch forward, two inches back. Could she just shove the letter at him, apologise for her mother, and leave it at that? She hadn't decided anything by the time she fell asleep.

The wretched letter. Perhaps she ought to throw it away. She reached into her pocket for it—it wasn't there.

She was hunting furiously through her bag when Pauline sailed in, all smiles.

'You look as though you've lost a pound and found a penny,' she said breezily to Leigh. Daphne frowned, but she was still gratified from the birthday gift, and said nothing.

'Happy birthday, Daph!' said Pauline, placing a package on her desk.

Leigh was going quietly berserk. Where could she have dropped the letter? She had had it when she'd gone down to breakfast, she knew that. She'd checked, because she had no intention of letting her mother know about it just yet. Could she have dropped it in her car? She would slip out as soon as she had a spare moment during the handicapped children's class.

It wasn't there. Pauline hadn't noticed she'd gone—she was too busy talking to the physiotherapist about a little boy with cerebral palsy. Leigh was on tenterhooks until the clinic was over, and hurried out before anyone could delay her.

Graham wasn't there. Evelyn, feeling much better, and coughing much less, was pottering around upstairs in her dressing-gown. Surreptitious glances around the hall and on the stairs and landing revealed nothing. They went down to the kitchen, Evelyn making

223

suggestions for her lunch.

'I feel like a little cheese on toast. Perhaps some mushroom soup.'

They both saw the letter at the same time, on the floor near the fridge. Evelyn was nearer and picked it up, but instantly Leigh grabbed it from her hand.

'It's rude to snatch,' said Evelyn plaintively. 'Anyway, how do you know it's yours?'

'I dropped it this morning.' Leigh pushed it in her pocket and turned to open a can of soup.

'There isn't a stamp on it—I noticed that,' said her mother, sitting at the table. 'It must have been delivered by hand.'

'I know who it's from,' said Leigh, stirring. 'I think we need more cheese.'

She turned to lay the table, and found Evelyn with the letter in her hand, staring at it.

'Mother, that was private. You took it from my pocket!' She reached out for it. Her mother didn't speak, just stared at it, her face pale. Leigh sat opposite her.

'I remember,' said Evelyn. 'I remember it all now.' Leigh waited. The gas hissed under the soup, and she turned it down.

'Headaches—terrible headaches,' said Evelyn slowly. 'And sickness. I left it as long as I dared, then I went to see Dr Williams. He wasn't there. It was a young doctor with fair hair—far too young to be a doctor, I thought.'

'Adam Christie,' Leigh prompted her.

Evelyn seemed to have forgotten she was there.

'Yes, Dr Christie. He asked me questions. Said it could be a number of things. He thought the best thing for me would be to see a specialist. He wrote a letter for me, there and then—said it would be quicker that way. I remember watching him as he wrote it. He had nice handwriting. He told me to ring the outpatient department at the Queen Anne and make an appointment to see the man on the letter as soon as possible—Mr Jephcott.'

'But you didn't,' said Leigh softly. 'Why not?'

'I was frightened. He was so very young. I thought he couldn't possibly know what was wrong. It was just eye-strain, I thought. Yet he hadn't even mentioned that. And then I thought why did he want me to go to the hospital so quickly? It had to be because he suspected something dreadful. It made me scared. I didn't want to know. I didn't want to die!'

'Oh, Mother!' Leigh could imagine her mother's secret anguish.

'I didn't know when Dr Williams would be back. I had faith in Dr Williams. I thought if I waited a bit I might start to feel better. He'd given me some pain-killers, and if they didn't work I'd go and see Dr Williams when he came back.'

'Did you start to feel better?' Leigh had to

225

say something.

'Only for a week or two. So I decided to ring the hospital after all. And I couldn't find the letter. I'd put it in a safe place, so no one else would find it, and I couldn't remember where. I didn't like to go back to Dr Christie and admit that I hadn't done as he'd said.'

'He might not have been there,' Leigh pointed out. 'He was just a locum.'

'I didn't know that. I was in a dilemma. I knew I was getting worse. I'd decided to go to the doctor that evening, the day I went into town. I wasn't feeling very well, and shouldn't really have gone, but it was Kate's birthday, and I hadn't bought her anything . . . I don't remember what happened after that.'

'You lost your balance, or went dizzy, or something, I expect,' said Leigh.

Evelyn nodded. She looked up from the letter. 'I've spoiled it all for you, haven't I? I told him he was making excuses, inventing this letter. I told him you'd believe anything he told you, because you were in love with him. I think it upset him. I can't think why I was so cruel. What can I do to make amends?'

She looked so woebegone that Leigh felt quite distressed. She gave her an emotional hug, her throat tight. The soup was starting to boil, and she turned off the gas.

'You'll show him the letter, won't you?' asked Evelyn. 'And tell him how sorry I am for not believing him?'

'I'm not sure it will make any difference now,' sighed Leigh.

'He's in love with you. That's why what I said hurt him so.'

'I'm not so sure,' said Leigh. 'Let's have our lunch. Where's the cheese?'

*   *   *

Back at the centre she sorted out her visits for the afternoon. A primary in Byron Walk, the maisonettes. A couple in the tower blocks in Shelley Crescent. The child with brittle bones in Eliot Road. Her hand hesitated over Kim Fletcher's card, then she added it to her pile. Oh, yes, and she was visiting the little deaf boy in Mouse Lane, so Pamela Varley could be seen briefly.

She put on her coat. If Adam wasn't here now, he was bound to be here when she got back.

Because the weather had improved, and the sun was shining temporarily, no one seemed to be at home. Everywhere she saw mothers pushing prams and strollers. She eventually reached the Varley house in Mouse Lane. Pamela opened the door.

'How are you?' asked Leigh, stepping into the hall.

Pamela gave a wry smile. 'Not so bad. Cup of tea?' She exuded an aura of excitement, and Leigh wondered what had happened.

227

'No, thank you, Pamela, I can't stop. I came to talk about counselling.'

Pamela beamed at her. 'Oh, but there's no need. I've got some wonderful news. I'm pregnant.'

'So soon? Are you sure?'

'I had a test. I thought all that sickness I had was the shock of the miscarriage, but it wasn't. You see, I do really want a baby. Carl and I, we've been doing a lot of talking, and I think I've finally laid the ghost of Matthew's death. I can see now I've been torturing myself for years. If only someone had told me what you did. I'm so glad you came. And I just know I shan't lose this one. I've got a feeling about it.' Her smile was ecstatic.

'So you don't need me any more,' said Leigh. 'Although I'll have to keep in touch. And when I see you in a few months' time I'm sure it will be for a happier reason.'

'I'll call her after you—if it's a girl!'

Leigh laughed and got into her car, and drove along to Eliot Road. Susan Fletcher was gazing out of the window when Leigh arrived. She seemed surprised to see her.

'Kim's at nursery school,' she explained as they sat down.

'It's you I've come to see. I was passing this way, and I remembered we didn't have time to finish our conversation yesterday.'

Susan seemed quite unsuspicious of this explanation. 'Oh, at the centre. Well, you'd have laughed. I felt such a fool. It wasn't a lump at all, it was a rib!'

'A rib? Well, that's a good thing, isn't it?' smiled Leigh. 'I mean, all these things you've had wrong with you lately, but fortunately none of them has turned out to be serious.'

She watched Susan's reaction. The girl bit her lip and looked awkward.

'Susan, what's really wrong?' Leigh asked.

'I told you—nothing. Just a rib. That's if she was right, and not trying to fob me off.'

'I'm sure Dr Powell wouldn't do that. Did you really think it was something serious?'

Susan's shoulders seemed to sag. 'I don't want to be thirty-nine,' she said in a low voice. 'It's an awful age.'

Leigh tried desperately to remember the clues Susan must have given her on the first visit. She had been—yes—seventeen when her mother died. Her mother must have been quite young . . .

'Susan, was your mother thirty-nine when she died?' she asked.

The girl's mouth dropped open. She nodded. 'Everyone says I'm the living image of her. She got cancer. It was awful. I keep thinking I shall die at the same age, next year. And I can't—I have three young children. Oh, it isn't logical, is it?'

'Logic doesn't come into it,' said Leigh. 'Not where your emotions and fears are concerned. All right, so you look like your mother, but it doesn't follow you're going to have all her illnesses. Chances are you'll live to a ripe old age.'

'I know—I try to tell myself that. Then I get frightened. Every little pain I get, every twinge, I imagine— What can I do?'

'First you go to see Dr Christie, tell him how you feel, and why. Ask him to refer you to someone who can help you. Psychotherapy, perhaps. Will you do that?'

Susan nodded.

'Right, let's have a cup of coffee, shall we?'

*   *   *

The visits took longer than Leigh had intended. She'd had coffee with Susan Fletcher, and the woman had wanted to talk, so Leigh was not surprised when she got back to the centre after five o'clock to find Adam had already left.

She wasn't sure rehearsal evening was the best time to approach him about Colin, and the letter, but realised she would be too tense to put herself into her part if it was still all on her mind. She would show him as soon as she saw him, apologise for her mother, and see how he took it.

At home, Graham had turned up again and was busy in the kitchen, concocting some fancy dish to tempt Evelyn's appetite. It was a sort of chicken and prawn soufflé with toasted breadcrumbs and celery, and, despite her mounting anxiety, Leigh quite enjoyed it. Graham certainly seemed to have hidden talents!

She didn't bother dressing up for the evening, just slipped on her black jumper over her jeans, brightened up with a narrow red scarf tied loosely around the polo neck.

Adam wasn't there when she arrived, which deflated her determination somewhat. The letter seemed to be burning a hole in her jeans pocket.

Roger seemed anxious to get started, and chose a scene with Leigh, Sarah, and Mark in it to begin. It was during the scene that Leigh noticed the hall doors quietly open, and Adam came soft-footed across the floor towards them. His fair hair was tousled, giving him a boyish look, and Leigh stumbled over her words in the rush of desire that suddenly seemed to envelop her. She forgot her words, and had to use her book, and she knew he must be watching her, his eyes laughing at her as they always used to.

The scene over, she returned to the floor and sat next to him. She wanted to tell him about Colin, to reassure him . . .

'On stage, Adam,' called Roger. Leigh tried to relax as she watched them rehearse, but all she could think of was the way he'd looked at her yesterday, the words he had spoken. No trust, no relationship. But she did trust him!

Then it was time for a break, and there was no chance to tell him, as she listened with the others while he explained why he'd been late, and looked a mess.

'I was on my way here, I'd stopped at Lear Terrace for the traffic to go round the island, and someone started pulling at the passenger door and banging on the glass. I recognised her as one of my patients, a young woman with a toddler, and she was looking desperate.'

'She wanted a lift, perhaps?' joked someone, and was quickly shushed.

'Oh, no, she'd recognised me. It was medical help she wanted. So I drove round the corner, to the maisonettes in Byron Walk—you know them?'

There were murmurs of agreement. Everyone was hanging on his words.

'The child had swallowed a boiled sweet and was choking. The mother didn't know what to do. A friend who was with her—fortunately— had tried thumping the child's back, but with no success. She was still trying when we arrived, but was getting tired, and the child was unconscious.'

'Oh, my goodness!' someone exclaimed. Leigh held her breath.

'It was just a matter of doing an abdominal thrust manoeuvre,' said Adam matter-of-factly. 'And bingo! The sweet popped out, and the child started to come round.'

There was a moment of silence, then they

all began talking at once.

'What a bit of luck for her that she saw you at the lights,' said Roger.

'It was,' Adam agreed. 'The phone box in Byron Walk was out of order, and she was rushing along to the one in Shakespeare Way. I doubt if the ambulance would have got there in time.'

The enormity of this took a moment to sink in, then Sarah said, in a breathy voice, 'It must make you feel wonderful, saving a life like that.'

'That's the whole point,' said Adam. 'Anyone can learn it. But yes, it is a nice feeling. Isn't it, Leigh?'

Suddenly everyone's gaze was on her. She flushed, remembering that day in Stow. She nodded. 'Yes, it's a nice, warm feeling.'

She went to put her empty cup on the table. She wished Adam hadn't looked at her like that, with faint reproach in his eyes. Was he still feeling disappointed in her?

She felt a hand on her shoulder, and her pulse quickened. But it was just Roger, exhorting them to hurry as they had a lot to get through.

The last scene of the evening was between Celia and Rupert. Leigh tensed as she sat on the stage waiting for Adam's entrance. He came in very softly and stood behind her. His hand stroked her hair, and a shudder went through her. She stood up to face him.

'You came back,' she said.

'I had to. I don't know what you're planning to do, Celia. All I want to do is hurt you the way you've hurt me.'

'Rupert, I'm sorry—I never meant—'

He spoke harshly, grasping her shoulders roughly. 'Of course you meant it! You meant every part of that devious little trick! And to think I loved you once—' His voice thrilled with emotion. He pulled her to him, crushing her in his arms until she could hardly breathe.

'Rupert, you must let me explain—'

His breath was hot on her face. 'Do you think I'd believe one word of it? Don't even try. This is what I think of your explanation!'

His lips pressed against hers fiercely, almost painfully, making her want to cry out, but she couldn't breathe. She struggled to get free, and suddenly he released her. They were both breathing hard. Leigh collapsed into the nearest chair.

Then Sarah entered, blinking her doe eyes at him, and Adam played up to her charms while Leigh sat in the corner, remorseful and sad. Finally the other two left amid laughter and kisses, and Leigh was left on the stage, in tears.

'My God!' said Roger, approaching her. 'Real tears! Fantastic!'

Leigh gave a tremulous smile, hardly registering Adam's look of concern. Of course they were real tears; she had felt Adam's anger

234

and pain in his kiss, and they too had been real. How could things ever come right again?

They started to collect their things together. Adam was talking to Roger. Leigh waited, tense, for them to finish. Finally Roger moved away, talking to Sarah, and they dawdled across the floor to the exit. Adam put on his jacket, turning to see that Leigh was still there, fiddling with her bag and looking uncomfortable.

'Did you want me, Leigh?' he asked, and she couldn't read the strange expression on his face. But what a silly question! Did she want him!

'Adam, I've found something—and I want to explain—' She was almost echoing the words of the play. She pulled out the crumpled letter and held it out to him. He stared at it, but didn't take it, a wry expression crossing his face.

'The letter.' The words seemed to echo in the empty hall. The footsteps of the others faded away.

'I didn't know whether I should just throw it away, forget I'd found it—but Mother saw it, and she remembered how it happened—'

'And now you feel you can trust me. Is that what you're trying to say? That now you've found the letter you have proof that I was telling the truth?'

'No, Adam—'

'You obviously didn't hear what I said

yesterday, after your mother had told me a few home truths. If a relationship needs proof to give it existence then it's no relationship at all. I had hoped—I had thought once that you might—' Adam's face suddenly twisted with emotion. Leigh wanted to put her arms round him, to ease the hurt away, but the expression in his eyes made her back away.

'Please, Adam,' she whispered.

His lips tightened. 'I think you'd better go, Leigh. Just go.' His voice was ominously quiet. He turned away from her, the set of his shoulders tense. Her throat choked with emotion, Leigh almost ran from the hall. Why would he never listen to her reasons? Did he think she was another Fenella? She paused in the foyer, fighting back the tears. She clenched her fists. All right, so it was the end of the relationship, but it wasn't the end of her life. There would be someone else, someone just as nice . . .

I refuse to plead with anyone, she vowed. I refuse to beg his forgiveness. It wasn't my fault. Angrily she crushed the letter in her fist and flung it in the nearest waste-bin. Holding her head high, blinking back the tears, she left the building.

The street was dark. The nearest streetlamp was unlit. Her car— Was that someone waiting by her car? No, not waiting—bending over the lock, trying to steal it! Adrenalin surged through her, and instinctively she ran towards him.

'Hey, what do you think you're doing? That's my car!'

The would-be thief was young, unkempt, and smelled of beer. As Leigh reached him, thrusting out a hand, he suddenly lashed out, knocking her off balance. She fell heavily to the pavement, jarring her wrist. The youth grabbed at the strap of her bag, but she refused to let go. Struggling, she was only vaguely aware of a fist coming towards her face.

It didn't land. The youth was suddenly flung away from her, and she heard Adam's angry voice. But her assailant was wiry, and he twisted out of Adam's grasp, running hell for leather up the street and out of sight.

'He's got away,' Leigh said weakly, as she struggled to her feet. Adam's arm was around her, and it felt strong and comforting.

'He doesn't matter. You're most important. Are you all right?'

'Yes—no—I don't know. My wrist—'

He held it with firm, experienced fingers, touching and pressing.

'I don't think it's broken. Perhaps we ought to get it X-rayed to be on the safe side.'

The tenderness and concern in his voice suddenly broke down her defences, and tears began to stream down her cheeks.

'Leigh—Leigh, what is it? Oh, please don't cry like that!'

'I'm sorry—I'm sorry—it's just— Hold me, Adam, just hold me!'

His arms came out and enfolded her and she wept against his tweed coat. He murmured words of consolation, and slowly her sobbing ceased. She sniffed, and fumbled for a handkerchief.

'You're shocked,' said Adam. 'Come on, let's sit in my car, then I'll take you home.'

'Someone might steal mine,' she said weakly, as he led her to his car.

'We'll worry about that later.'

They sat next to each other in the dark, and, even though she still felt shaken, Leigh couldn't stop excitement stirring in her veins.

'Why did you tell me to go?' she whispered. He didn't answer for a moment. She could hear his breathing, she heard him swallow.

'I was afraid,' he admitted.

'Afraid?'

'Afraid and proud. Afraid to let you see how much I needed you, afraid you'd see my weakness. And too proud to admit I'd been arrogant and stubborn.'

'My mother says we're both stubborn,' said Leigh softly.

'Your mother's right. And there was something else I was afraid of. I was afraid you might stop loving me, might turn back to that Colin fellow in Bath— Oh, Leigh, please don't go back, stay here, with me! I was so afraid your mother was right about him. I should

238

have listened to you, believed you, trusted you.'

'She tried to make you jealous,' Leigh told him.

'And she succeeded. But it only made me afraid that you might—' He paused.

'Might hurt you, like Fenella?' she finished. 'Oh, Adam, you should have trusted me more. I did trust you, really I did, even over all that— I just always seemed to show it in the wrong way. Colin has never meant anything to me; no one meant anything until you came along. That first day, in Stow, I think I fell in love with you then. And that wretched letter, it almost ruined everything!'

'Your mother saw it?'

She nodded. 'It was a good thing, in a way. It made her remember almost everything— why she didn't go to the hospital. But Adam, I want to forget all that now. It only drove a wedge between us. I've thrown the letter away.'

'I saw you. And you can't imagine how I felt when I watched you walk away from me, and I knew I'd broken your heart. I thought I'd lost you forever, and that would have broken mine.' He kissed her nose. 'You've got a drip.'

She giggled and wiped it away. 'There's still something you haven't told me yet, Adam.'

His voice was low and intimate. 'What's that?'

'You've never said you were in love with

me.'

He drew back and looked at her. And the moon suddenly appeared from behind a cloud, and Leigh could see the love in his eyes. Her heart seemed to swell with answering emotion.

'Haven't I?' he murmured, stroking her neck gently, and sending an electric current through her body. 'How remiss of me. Perhaps I thought you knew. But no, how could you, when I've behaved like an absolute louse? Let me remedy it now. My personal prescription. Doctor's orders.'

He touched her lips softly with his, stirring her senses. 'I love you, I love you, I love you. Will that do for now?'

'Not yet,' she murmured, returning his kiss. 'Tell me again and again.'